To

fellow writer

Zohra

STUMBLING THROUGH

DARKNESS

with love,

Flavia Cosma

Toronto, Nov. 18, 2006

Stumbling Through Darkness

A Collection of Works

WINGATE PRESS
Ontario, Canada

ISBN 0-9780758-0-3

Layout design by Wingate Press
Cover Design by Wingate Press
Edited by Stacey Lynn Newman
Cover photograph by Stephen Newman

Published by:

Wingate Press
www.wingatepress.com

We acknowledge the support of the Canada Council for the Arts
which last year invested $20.0 million in writing and publishing throughout Canada.

Canada Council   Conseil des Arts
for the Arts   du Canada

Printed in Canada

Stumbling Through Darkness

Table of Contents

INTRODUCTION

Writers are as different from one another as bushes and trees in a forest. Some reach for the sky. Some hear the music of the bluebell roots. Each is part of the variety, the complex ecology and health of the forest. I feel that we are particularly blessed in Canada to have a populace that reads, to have people who write, and a world that welcomes what we have to say.

When I was in Israel about two decades ago, attending a conference for women writers, a visit to a kibbutz was arranged. A lone writer lived there. One of our group asked him how he could survive as a writer without the stimulus of other writers. He replied that only a writer could receive sustenance from any situation. I have sometimes thought of that remark when I find myself feeling rather alone or adrift and discover that the air is teeming with language, with stimulus and communication. Some of it comes from books.

Congratulations to the authors whose works are contained in this anthology. May your readership find the sustenance here that feeds the hunger for meaning.

And may I take this opportunity too, to thank the Canadian Authors Association for choosing *Obasan* as their Book of the Year when it was published in the 80's.

Joy Kogawa

Poetry

Fay Manawwar

Jurassic Park

If you go down to Jurassic Park
You better not go alone
Take your stick in your hand
And tap on every stone

When walking through the
forest
Don't leave your Nani's hand
Poke your stick in the ground
And check for sinking sand

The fossils in Jurassic Park
Will glisten in the dark
Look, Heidi goes ahead of you
And signals with a bark

When searching for those Dino
eggs
Hidden among the rocks
The red ants army will attack
So wear your shoes and socks

Be careful of the Dino dung
It's Nana's biggest treasure
If you put your foot in it
He'll jump for joy with
pleasure

Requiem in Jurassic Park

Now Joshua is in Jurassic Park
He lies among the brave
White lilies grow beside him
Green grass upon his grave

The Dinos weep in sorrow
For Joshua they did adore
"He was our Monach and
King."

No bulbul sings, no koel calls
Silent the sun bird and the
dove
The red ants stand in mute
salute
For Joshua now in heaven
above

Train to Melshedore

O have you got your tickets
On the train to Melshedore?
It's ready at the platform
And leaves at half past four

The engine driver's standing
In his coat of navy blue
His hand is on the whistle cord
To make it call "choo choo."

The furnace is blazing
As the fireman shovels coal
With hissing steam the pistons push
And make the big wheels roll

The guard has shown the green flag
The signal's dipping down
O hurry Jems and Ryan
You'll be left behind in town

Sit by the window, we're moving
Can you hear the tree tops roar?
Let's eat our chocolate Tim-Tams
On the train to Melshedore.

Limericks and Medicos

A short little lady, Miss Small named White
Paid the wise Dr. Long a call
She complained with a sigh: "I am as short as a fly."
And very soon she was long and not small

There was a blood corpuscle
Who by nature was a true phagocyte
Once he forgot who he was and this is the cause
Of the mysterious disappearance of White

A bold bad bacterium named Bill
Came and sat on a window sill
Now the maid, poor lass who cleaned the same glass
From the doctor received a new bill

A dashing young doc from Vellore
Got a call at just half past four
The situation was tough, he said
"I've had enough, so I'll return when half has passed four."

There was a young doctor named Phil Pott
Who thought he knew a terrible lot
He claimed he did see an appendix on the knee
Now it's for you to believe it or not

Sentimentalia Geriatrica

I love scraps of paper
And old greeting cards
Bits of used pencils
And scribbling of bards

Old pins and broaches
Broken or not
Tarnished or varnished
I treasure the lot

I hoard little pieces
Of ribbons and strings
Used wrapping papers
And such mundane things

No diamonds, no rubies
No pieces of jade
I treasure old things
Of the bygone decade

I love old clothes
And my old cushioned chair
I love my old friends with
Thinning gray hair

Enid Chan

My Family: The Past

Chan Chok Kwun, grandpa, the head of the clan
Came from a village in China with all the Chans
Way back in the 19th century
In Tangra, Calcutta started a factory

Grandpa with his brothers five
Unfortunately none of Dad's brothers did survive
Dad studied engineering in USA
Became an alcoholic but didn't join AA

Mom's brothers and sisters came to India during the war
During the 'partition' in the riots many slayings we saw
After India's independence, grandpa returned to Canton
But had to be rescued from the Cultural Revolution

The whole clan lived in a big red mansion
With orchards, fish pond and room for expansion
Soon the place was falling apart
So we decided to depart

Father decided to call it a day
Each of us siblings sailed away
Now we are settled over the seven seas
Some of us with our own families

My Family: The Present

Eleanor got married first, she is the eldest
Minna and Grace were nurses trained in the West
Enid, a doctor in Hong Kong loves sailing
Peter the youngest studied electrical engineering

Peter and Dawn in UK in bonsai excelled
Eleanor and Foowing: retired, have stories from Tripoli to tell
Grace, Kiong and Sharon live in Singapore
Minna has a degree from U of T; Enid now on Lake Ontario's
shore

In Bhutan live cousin Sunchair and her family
Next year cousin Annie will be ninety
Ah Kee had many daughters and sons
Tracing the rest of the relatives will be fun

Sharon, Shirley and Phillip in the world of finance
Justyn and Angela in the arts prefer to freelance
Eleanor's grandson Brandon, the youngest, is a baby
Up to the year 2006, this is my family

Nina

Nina is a child of God
Innocent as can be
With loving parents, sisters
And little nephews three

To the world's problems oblivious
She is blessed indeed
Her days go by in leisure
God and her family supply her needs

Fearfully and wonderfully made are we
If she could think, she'd ask "Why me?"
God in his wisdom does not explain

He doesn't mind if we complain

Even in the Book of Job
Job thought God was unfair
When chromosomes were given
Nina got three of chromosome 21 instead of a
pair

Trust God when he sends you your child
He'll also give strength, hope and love
Show you compassion, give you care
And look to him above.

Resident Bard of Christian Medical College, Vellore

Way back in the days of yore
In the sleepy town of Vellore
To study medicine the place to be
Was the revered institution of CMC

In the campus grounds barren as a rock
The shuttle buses trundled around the clock
Before seniors we would stand in awe
The study of anatomy and physiology a bore

Examination time: the common room was a scene
Nodding heads over medical books
Somnambulant zombies in every cranny and nook
During coffee breaks all day and night
Any knowledge of diagnosis of treatment took flight
Befuddled brains awoke to the chatter
Of our aspiring poet's prolific product of her gray matter

Many years down memory lane
Still ring the nostalgic refrain of Fay's poems
Now scattered the world all over
CMC's alumni exchange e-poetry in each other's homes

Katherine

Katherine Irwin, pastor of WUC
Alpha plus group leader and she
Teaches us lessons from the Bible and shares
Her life experiences with us who care

Eva, Janet, Enid, Brenda, Kae, Jean, Betty, and Sophie
Read the Bible, sing hymns and we
International cuisine enjoy
Nice memories we cherish with joy
Every one of us wishes her a happy retirement

fay: Her Dog's Doc

Fay is her dog's doc
In plain dog talk
Kruger said "Bow Wow"
She gave him medicine in his chow

Treated his paw
That was sore
She gave him antibiotics
Dressed his wounds under anaesthetic

At the end she looked pale
And had to take Adam's ale

Enid Chan, a doc in Gynae/Ob
Night and day women she would see
In Labour ward or gynaecology
Deliver babies or perform laparotomy

Christian service in Hong Kong
Hospital situated in Kwun Tong
A career Christ centred
Not to be ministered unto, but to minister

Bianca Lakoseljac

Do I Know Your Secret?

"Come with me
And all will be forgiven,"

You said as you took my hand
And led me to the white light
Acceptance knowledge wisdom of ages   love

Did you trust in me?
That I would not reveal your riddle
That I would not betray the labour
Of philosophers who gifted you one life after another
All the lives you hold captive in your white light

I said "no"

You dropped my hand
I fell with a thump
I am still here on respite

Amid essence and existence
Inadequacy of human reason
Waltzing clumsily the ancient rites of common destiny
Searching for the sacrament of beauty
Waiting for the promise in the white light

Do I know your secret?

The Prophecy

"Lonely in rain
Sadly in his sleep
He awaits for you

The man with blue eyes
Guarding the almanac of your culture
Fulfilling the prophecy
Demystifying biblical allusions"

Unified
We drift in the amniotic fluid
In the ambivalence of Siren and White Night

The tenor and the vehicle of a metaphor
Lending themselves to elaborate conceits
Controlling images of metaphysical poets
Discordia concors—concordia discours?
Metathesis yielding to spoonerism
Fulfilling the prophecy
Demystifying biblical allusions

Flawless in our limitations

'Til peath do us dart

Flawless thereafter

Family Jewels

You looked down
Handling them gingerly
Fluttering your slender fingers

Bathed in holy water
Clean like innocence

Eight is a magic number
For little boys
For future heroes

Deconstructing prose poems
Nonfiction novels
A modern invention
An ancient phenomenon

Proving worthy of the magic sword
Forged by the great Wayland

Are these our family jewels?
You asked

Yes
I answered
To be treasured
Always beautiful family jewels

Hours of Idleness

We ran outside holding hands
Lightning far away

Rain washing our salty naked bodies

The smile on your face
The giggle in your voice
The grace of your twirl
Hours of idleness lamenting the fleeting childhood

The golden age of light verse
Fanciful in delight

We danced in circles
Thunder rumbling in the distance
Nearer

You, hanging tightly to the fairy's tail for a bumpy ride
Through Astral planes
Foreseeing the sacred gifts
An apple from Avalon
A crystal of pure moonlight

Accept these gifts of the heart
Graciously, our daughter

Eternally

Waiting for the Phoenix

Rose thorns
Opious hyacinths
Latent rays of the setting sun
The glitter in the shimmering water
Moped up my ashes

A sandpiper pecked
The stray crumb

A silent sea gull
Sang my lullaby

My keening
Lifted the stardust
Uncovering the sacred burial ground

Undaunted as any muse you stood by
Tenaciously
The spiritual catalyst
While I sacrificed my triumph
Drifting in your sea of collective unconscious

I am sleeping
Sleeping
Waiting for the Phoenix

Flavia Cosma

These poems are translated from Romanian by the
author with Charles Siedlecki.

Manege Aquatic

Steely horses
Lather on the high seas;
The mind dozes off at the shores;
There is so much peace in helplessness,
The pain cannot pass through,
Neither can the dream.
Translucent walls shelter
The sleep of the unborn.

Gipsy women with hair painted yellow and blue
Lean naked by a tasselled camel,
Between its large humps
A monkey shrieks piercingly,
Boisterous children throng around,
Life lets itself be carried forward
As if it were a banner.

The wave forgets to return to shore,
The sea, a huge pail, waits
For better days.

In the Afternoon

An alder quivers
With its slender branches.
A rock rises lazily
Baking in the sun;
On the road a dog
Pulls its master along
As if carrying a load.

You pine-trees, tell me again
Those light Fairy Tales,
And you wind, send your golden fingers
Sifting through my hair.

Under the fiery eye
Girls change into flowers,
Flowers twist into garlands,
Birds smarten up
For the celebrations.

On silky skies
Clouds fall contentedly asleep;
Profound dreams shelter
The heart – a young bride.

The Lesson

The kids learn the taste of warm blood
In their primordial, solar rhythms;
They frolic on the plains, mating,
Without knowing that they are learning everything,
In front of everybody,
All at once.

Sculpture

The Genii are sculpting the stone
                    as if
They were seeing themselves in a mirror;
Now and then meek faces
Appear from a cloud;
Waves mould the depths of the sea
In their own images.

Shaped like dogs and infants,
Red stones lie under our soles,
Sharing with us their serene quiet.
A chubby angel smiles happily
From a heavenly corner of a garden.

So many beings vie with each other,
Watching us from the other world,
Mindful, they urge us on our paths,
Leading us gently by the hand.

The Rain Descends

The rain descends on ardent, boiling lakes,
Little golden coins tossed from shaken braids,
Salvers spread out shifting
On feverish, idle waters.

The rain descends, a softhearted bride,
into this thoughtless mist;
She enters, pure and trusting
into the hot and hungry waves.

Liisa Hypponen

**In memory of Tsunami victims
of December 26, 2004**

Sitting by the seashore at early dawn
Paradise all around
Turquoise water gently reaches towards me
And tenderly kisses my toes.

A deep sorrow washes over me
I hang my head and weep
Percolating from deep within
A cry of grief escapes my throat.

As mother earth cried out
That fearsome day in paradise
A rolling wave of anguish from her heart
Innocently carried thousands to a watery grave.

Birth of my father

Shadows beckon me in the graveyard
To my father's tomb
Where his body lay after all these years
Unidentifiable, in a satin womb

Though his flesh is decomposed
And time taken him away
His love lives within my heart
Each and every day

He is the man who showed me truth
And led me on my way
Who taught me to know right from wrong
When weak begged me to stay

As the shadows dissipate
My heart it comes quite clear
Though his body lay in a satin tomb
His spirit, alive, is near.

Daughter's Poem

Your eyes they shine with a deep inner light
The aura around you is a beautiful sight
Be strong and be true as you start your flight
And love will surround you through every dark night.

Cry when you're hurting and let it be so
Don't keep it inside, in time it will show
Fear not for tomorrow, nor regret the past day
For God gave you His blessing when He led you this way.

My darling young daughter your beauty is strong
Your mind is clear and your abilities long
So go on your journey, the path will unwind
And your spirit will keep you in great peace of mind.

Margo Georgakis

The Broken Tribesman

I made the pilgrimage
To the sacred ladder where
The river god transformed
You
From image to man.

Your eyes bound me to
An unremembered past.

Your arms reassured me of
Acceptance.

Your kiss held
Premonitions of betrayal.

I crossed the blurred threshold.
Future to past.
Death to birth.
Resurrection to crucifixion.

With broken spirit
I made the pilgrimage
To the sacred ladder
Hoping to reclaim
Me.

The Birthing Chair

The birthing chair began to rot,
As it remained in the garden of
Misplaced trust.

Infested by betrayal,
Its shaky surface sustained her
On the night of her labour.

Darkness fell.

He vanished with the sun
Choosing to claim
His freedom.

Waves struck the rocky shores.
Unrelenting waves purged her
From her fear of abandonment.

Deliberately, defiantly
She bound two wooden crosses
To the sacred oak.

One for her failed judgment
And the other for the birthing chair.

Michalaki (Greece 1947)

Pick them up!
Pick up his pieces.
Put his pieces on your apron.

Run! Run home!
Stop your begging.

His heart. Small, torn pieces.
Count them. One, two, three.

His cotton shirt.
Strands of his hair, walnut brown.

No food. No food.
Your husband owns no land.
Too proud to beg.
He sends you.

Only one eye found.
Light green.
Kissed both this morning.

He picked up the toy.
The toy that killed him.
No toys, no toys for your child.
Only grenades and land mines.

Nancy L. Hull

SHORELINE STUDY IN FOUR

I. Merganser Night

last night
we skimmed through woodland waters
parting veils of cedar-scented shadows
our sleek feathers beaded with liquid pieces
of a broken moon

hushed by hauntings of the
invasive species

we paused at a soft-spoken shoreline
sudden stillness in our valiant crests
absorbed images of a waterfowl kin
lifeless   suspended
amongst arched reeds and purple shrouds
mouth agape with human prints
a plastic ring had noosed its neck

II. Merganser Sunrise

a sorrel sunrise
welcomes our lucid silhouettes
we swim   we dive   we feed
we surface to cherish luscious
landscapes
of northern quietude   until

watchful waters cease our songs

alerting us to non-organic roars of
marauding bullies
humans and their angry engines
harass us in sadistic sport
or jealousy
clashing   crashing into frenzied waves
scalding speeds
that burn our hearts for escape

forcing us from our hallowed homes

III. Merganser Sunset

we gather
beneath marbled skies that rise
into an aureate chorus
echoed in glassy wetlands

linear outlines of our long thin beaks
are clues to cautious navigation
within this paradoxical paradise

we slip silently   struggling
through chemical compounds
perfect poisons   pesticides
unseen pools of slithery toxins
dumped surreptitiously by
invasive species
those humans who leave a legacy
of razor-edged tears

IV. Shoreline Search

beleaguered   bewildered
our gifted eyes seek into that species
violating our balanced north

the humans   so disconnected
in toxic selfishness
souls disintegrated
shattering lives
battering beauty
to eradication

the moon lies broken
scattered across our heavy lake

but maybe
in the distance
where wise pines
reach to timeless night skies
a silvery star
beckons

Pat Hart

Promises, Promises

God, in various forms promises many things.
The Christian God promises Heaven or Hell,
graphically illustrated and documented.

The Muslim Allah promises Paradise,
again with much poetic imagery.

Buddha offers Nirvana, or in some cases
endless reincarnations until one gets it right.

The list goes on and on through centuries
of pain, confusion and misunderstanding.

What insufferable arrogance of those
who claim the "One Truth!"

What appalling inhumanity of those
who kill to prove their cause!

What gross stupidity of those
who blindly follow!

What mute despair of those
who watch the madness!

Do we not read?
Do we not think?
Do we not care?

The Nude

The class enters the studio
with chalks and papers
and settles into place.
The lights are set.
We wait.

She is young, and as she sits
her long hair falls softly
defining her shoulders
and delicate breasts.
We draw.

Quietly we seek the form,
to catch the thrust of thigh
the turn of hand
the tilt of head
We rest.

She folds her body within her robe
and now is more than form.
She has a name.
The spell is broken
until she sits again.

Cowslips and Blackbirds

Winter debris smothers the marsh.
Broken spears of bulrushes pierce
this matted growth covering
the dark, wet soil.

Silently, from this dark, wet soil
through the matted growth,
cowslips surge in a burst
of fat green leaf.

Clusters of yellow flowers,
like patches of sunlight
glow in the cool, quiet
of the undergrowth.

Redwing blackbirds arrive
to perch on the bulrushes
shattering the silence,
announcing spring.

Jake Hogeterp

Epiphany

They clobbered me
in the foggy predawn coming to –
three everyday words, stitched together
by a devilishly clever array of prepositions
into a heart-stopping revelation.

Such joyous certainty they brought –
only to slow-dissolve into oblivion.
And in their wake, a desperate grasping
at the fragmenting memory.
And then sadness and anger
at the loss.

Perhaps the aphorism was a gift
meant only for momentary illumination.
At least I hadn't seen
how it could have been hammered out
of my own meagre talent.
Maybe it was just too potent
for my custody. Or could it be
that I had suddenly been pegged
a too-reluctant Jonah?

There's nothing left
but this telling – a secondary happiness.
Though who knows
with what burden
I may otherwise have saddled you?

Prose

Heart Condition
by Aprille Janes

As the lake darkened to indigo, a loon's hysterical laughter echoed along the far shoreline and drifted through the open cottage window.

"Is Grampa really driving his house here?" Katy asked, her voice muffled by the nightie slipping over her blonde curls.

"Yup. It's a house on wheels." I smiled at her little-girl giggle.

"Will Gramma bring presents?"

"Probably."

After she settled herself and Grizzle the teddy bear, I pulled the old patchwork quilt over the two of them and kissed the top of Katy's head. "Now, go to sleep. You don't want to be tired tomorrow."

I closed the door just as Paul came out of Robbie's room and gave me a thumbs up. Mission accomplished. We returned to the campfire down by the shoreline

Settling back against him in the lounge chair, my fingertips rested lightly on the pulse in his wrist. Many nights I had fallen asleep with my hand against his chest, feeling his heart beat against my palm. His strength propped up my own.

"I'm still not sure this is such a good idea, Paul."

"What were you going to say when they asked to come? No?"

"We've always gone to their place. We could leave when things got rough. Now..."

"This motor home is your dad's dream."

"But a whole week! Mom never keeps it together more than three days."

"The motor home will give her a place to unwind." He kissed the top of my head. "Don't let her get to you."

I stiffened. "Easy for you to say."

"I can only tell you what you already know," Paul tightened his arms around me, pulling me back into his chest. "I stood up to her from day one and she leaves me alone. If you did, too, she'd back off."

35

"It was different for you. Your mother wasn't so...so unreasonable."

Paul sighed. "Look, let's not talk about her anymore. We're letting her ruin our vacation before she even gets here!"

Paul was right. I let it go and lay quiet in his arms listening to the wavelets lapping the shore. As the fire burned down to embers his hand drifted up to my breast and I turned my head to kiss the sweet, familiar taste of him. Without a word, he nudged me slightly with his shoulder and we went back up to the cottage.

Undressing each other in the dark, we took things slow. This was vacation. No alarm clocks for two weeks. Time enough for everything.

Afterwards, he rolled onto his back, wrapped one arm around me and pulled me against his side. I settled into his warmth as his breathing deepened and he drifted off to sleep. But I lay awake for a long time with one hand pressed against his heart.

***

Around 3 o'clock the next afternoon the four of us walked up the dirt lane. As we neared the corner Robbie ran ahead. "I'm going to see them first."

Katy dropped my hand and raced after him. "Me too, me too."

Paul and I sat on a sun-warmed boulder while the kids jockeyed for front position with shoulders and elbows until Paul called, "Enough you two."

Their patience was growing thin when the motor home finally arrived in a cloud of dust, my parents waving from behind a vast expanse of windshield. The kids jumped and pointed and and hollered, "They're here! They're here!"

They stayed at a cautious distance until the huge vehicle lumbered to a stop and Dad opened the door. Then, with cries of 'Grampa!' they ran over and clambered on board to ride the few hundred yards down our lane while Paul and I followed on foot.

When we caught up, Mom and the kids were already in the back surveying the booty piled high on the spare bunks. Snorkels and flippers, sand buckets and shovels, inflatable toys and rafts, new swimsuits and summer clothes. Mom and Christmas arrived in July.

Dad gave us the tour, opening cupboards, lifting seats, proudly showing off the tiny bathroom. "We're headed for Banff when we leave here."

"I'm glad for you." I hugged him, enjoying the familiar Old Spice, the feel of his slim shoulders, his strong arms. I whispered, "How's Mom?"

"Tired."

I hugged him again as the kids tumbled from the bunk room, arms laden with gifts. Mom followed, her short round figure silhouetted by sunlight from the window behind her.

"I see your father gets the first hug." She lifted her cheek for me to kiss while her arms remained at her side. "Well, let's go see this cottage you've been raving about."

As the men parked the motor home and the kids headed out back with their loot, I trailed my mother into the cottage for the inspection tour.

"How was your trip?" I tried to sound cheery and upbeat.

She checked out the bathroom and each bedroom before returning to where I waited in the living room. Studying the titles in the bookshelves, she finally answered, "Not bad. I can go in the back and sleep."

She peered out the window towards the small beach. "Do you think the kids like their gifts?"

"I'm sure they do. But you shouldn't have, you know."

At last she looked at me. "You barely let me see my grandchildren so don't be telling me what I should and shouldn't do."

I took a deep breath and let it out quietly before asking, "Did you have lunch?"

"I did but I'd like a cup of tea. With lemon," She settled onto the sofa, plumping a pillow behind her back. "My little kitchen has a microwave and everything but we'll eat our meals with you folks."

"We only eat two meals a day. A late breakfast and then an early supper. That won't work for you, will it? With your diabetes and all?"

Please, please.

"That sounds fine. I'll grab something in between if I need to. No reason to fuss over me."

***

By day three, the warning signals began flashing.

"Don't you know I need to eat at regular times?" she grumbled before digging into her sausage and pancakes. My stomach tightened into a too-familiar knot but I stifled my irritated reply. She finished eating in silence before disappearing back out to the motor home.

I watched the kids play all morning from a comfortable Muskoka chair on the back deck. Just before lunch, Robbie got bored and went looking for the men. Katy, with Grizzle tucked under one small arm, came over to me and asked, "Read to me, Mommy?"

"More Narnia?" She nodded and I reached down to pull the book out from under my chair.

Katy settled herself and Grizzle comfortably in my lap and with the lapping water as background music, our sunny deck seemed the perfect place for fantastic tales.

"Let's see, where did we leave off?"

In a few moments we were back among the talking animals of Narnia when Mom came around the corner and settled in the chair beside us. Without looking at me, she reached out her arms to Katy.

"Give Gramma a kiss."

"No," Katy snuggled closer to me, hugging Grizzle tighter.

Mom stood up and returned to the motor home.

At lunch when she didn't appear I asked, "Is Mom okay?"

Dad replied, "She's lying down. Headache, I think."

She didn't appear again until our mid-afternoon cruise to Big Buoy's Marina for ice cream. She spoke only in monosyllables as we crossed the lake but after we docked, she climbed out, took Robbie's hand and announced, "You're a good boy. Choose any candy you want and Gramma will get it for you."

Robbie looked surprised and then pleased as the two of them headed up the dock to the store.

Katy's stricken face cut to my heart. Before I could respond Dad moved forward and picked her up. "And you're a good girl. Come show Grampa what you want."

I started to follow but Paul touched my arm and held me back. When Dad and Katy were out of earshot he asked, "What's going on?"

"She's ticked off because Katy wouldn't kiss her."

"I'm not about to let her start on the kids."

"I don't think she will. A good night's sleep should fix things."

He didn't look convinced as we followed the others up to the marina store.

The next morning, I rose early and slapped bacon into the old frying pan. The delicious smell mingled with the aroma of fresh coffee. I squeezed oranges and furiously whipped eggs up for scrambling.

This is my vacation, too, dammit. I pulled out plates and slammed the cupboard door closed. *Just two more days. Please just get me through two more days.*

The screen door screeled open and my parents walked in. Dad kissed my cheek and sniffed appreciatively. "Smells good."

Mom didn't say a word, just sat down and poured herself a mug of coffee. A minute later the kids clattered in. Robbie hugged Mom around the neck and she patted his arm as he kissed her cheek. Right behind him came Katy, faithful Grizzle tucked under one arm.

Katie reached for Mom but my mother pushed her away, picked up her coffee and left. The screen door slapped shut. Katy's face crumpled and two large tears welled up.

The scrape of my father's chair across the worn tiles felt like nails on a chalkboard. "I'm sorry. I'll go see what I can do."

Paul banged down his coffee mug. "I'm not putting up with this any longer." He stood up and started towards the door.

I scooped up a crying Katy and intercepted my husband. "Wait a minute."

"No, I won't wait. This has to stop. Now."

"Yes, it does. And I'm the one that has to do it."

Paul looked doubtful but finally he put out his arms and took Katy from me.

Stalking out to the motor home, I yanked open the door where it flew out of my hand and banged against the side of the vehicle. My mother, seated in her rocker, looked up from a book while Dad sat nearby, his head in his hands. My voice sliced through the room. "Who the HELL do you think you are?"

Her dark eyes glittered. "You can't speak to me that way."

"You act like you're the centre of the universe. And we let you get away with it. Even as kids. Especially as kids."

"I was a good mother."

"You don't know the meaning of the word. You and your damn moods. I spent my whole, damn childhood trying to keep you happy. And it was hell."

"Watch your language."

"I'll swear if I damn well please."

Mom's face reddened and her eyes narrowed as I continued, "You're not going to start your games with my children. Do you understand? You're welcome to stay but new rules go into place today."

I turned to my father. "Daddy, I'm sorry but I have to protect the kids."

He whispered "It's okay, Honey. I understand."

I slammed the door shut behind me and walked around to our back deck. *The Lion, The Witch and The Wardrobe* lay open on the floor by my chair. Sitting down, I stared across the lake, waiting for the trembling in my legs to stop.

I expected to hear footsteps behind me, expected Mom to bring the battle to me. I waited but instead, the motor home's big engine roared to life about twenty minutes later. I tracked the sound as it disappeared down the laneway and out to the road.

When silence fell again, I buried my head on my arms and wept for a long time. I surrendered to the years of stored anger and frustration.

Finally, I grabbed a towel left to dry on the railing and dabbed at my eyes. A nearby balsam filled the air with Christmas perfume while somewhere out on the bay a loon laughed. Behind me, human laughter lured me back into the cottage.

Paul was serving scrambled eggs to the kids. When he spotted me in the doorway, he set the frying pan back on the stove and came over.

"I heard. Damn. Even the neighbours heard!"

Then, with one arm he pulled me close, placed his hand over my heart and kissed me.

Clash of Cultures

by Ben Antao

The dinner went off well, Vernon Rao felt, judging by the gusto
with which Clement Perry ate the spiced curried chicken breasts
and the saffron basmati rice. After dessert and coffee, with
brandy in their hands, he gently guided his colleague, a white
Canadian, back to the dining table, by now cleared of dishes, to
unburden his soul. Their wives chatted in the living room.

"I've been teaching for five years now, I am thirty-five and I
want to move into administration, but I feel stumped," said Rao
who preferred to go by his last name.

Clement, a social studies teacher in the same high school,
liked his Indian colleague very much, although with a touch of
envy, for Rao had three degrees—in English, math and business.

"Maybe, the problem is you're over-qualified," said Clem, his
blue eyes clear as a sky in September.

"You don't believe that!"

"It's not what I believe," said Clem, "but perception shapes
reality." Then he averted his eyes as if trying to remember
something. "Thought you were my age, thirty-one. You look a lot
younger."

Rao, a Christian immigrant from India, grinned and revealed
his perfectly set white teeth. "I've heard that comment before; it
seems brown skin doesn't age as fast."

Clem took another sip from the goblet. His round face above
his V-neck maroon cardigan and open white shirt collar glowed
like a baby's after the bath, pink and healthy-looking. His reddish
brown hair grown to a tangled mass at the nape of his neck. "I
don't think it's that really. You've got to know how the system
works and play your cards accordingly." He mused...*If I were in
his place I'd have been a VP by now. A shame he can't crack the
system. With such intelligence!* "You've got to get involved. Try
for department headship first—you're in three departments, for
crying out loud."

Rao pushed further, to get a feel for Clem's bias. "You think
they are going to make me head of English? Come on now, are

you patronizing me? If it's not the colour of my skin, it's my accent."

Clem lifted a package of cigarettes from inside his shirt pocket, and asked, "Do you mind?"

"Go right ahead. Be at home."

Clem lit a cigarette, turned outwards his pink lower lip to puff out, and said, "Have an idea for you. Why don't we discuss it sometime next week?"

The staff meeting was usually held in the morning prior to the start of school, but this one, in the last week of September, was special with just one item on the agenda—to elect a staff rep for their union. In the past, there had been no election as the same person agreed to carry on and was acclaimed. A day before the meeting, Clem met with Rao after school in his small history office. "Remember our little chat at your place?"

"Yes."

"I want you to become staff rep for our union," Clem began. "I've checked around, talked to a few people. And I think you should go for it. The current rep, whom I tried to persuade to step down, won't budge. He wants an election, and he'll get one. I'm going to nominate you. I've a seconder in place. All you need to do is tell the staff why you want to be the rep, and we'll take it from there. Okay?"

The way Clem made his pitch, Rao thought, left him with no option but to acquiesce. A sudden thrill warmed up Rao's spirit, like a burst of sunlight after an autumnal storm.

The meeting was held in the library, a large rectangular room, and some fifty-plus staffers trooped in, amidst groans and sighs of exhaustion. "I want to serve the staff as well as I am serving the students," said Rao. "It's my way of helping out my fellow teachers, and all I ask is your support. I'll do a good job, if you give me a chance, trust me."

The ballots were counted and Rao was declared the winner.

Back in their little office, Clem said, "This is the first step, remember, on the way to your dream. If autumn is here, can spring be far behind?"

"Thanks for everything," said Rao shaking hands. "You've got the quotation wrong, though, but the sentiment is right on. I appreciate it. It's winter, not autumn, according to Shelley."

"You're the English teacher."

***

In May the students go wild like the starlings and chickadees, chirping, twittering, bursting into a sudden, frenzied scattering from their winter nests in the high maples. Like the birds, the students can't wait to get out of the classroom, on to the field for soccer and baseball, to smell the fresh air, to gaze at the unfurling greenery, to hear their own changing voices, to touch and feel their pale skins in the spring sun, to wonder at their developing taste buds and how everything tastes different. It's a month of promise and Rao's spirits twittered and pulsed expectantly when he went to see the principal.

"How's it going? Have a seat," said the principal, a tall man in his fifties, with a lean frame that suggested he was genetically incapable of gaining weight, no matter how much he ate. "I've carefully studied your application for department headship. It looks good. There are two other candidates for the same position, equally qualified, and good." He studied Rao with those keenly daunting eyes that sent a shiver through the students whenever he walked into a classroom to confer briefly with the teacher.

"I'm listening," said Rao, holding the other's gaze.

"As you know, I must choose the best candidate, all things being equal."

"Is seniority any consideration?"

"I've thought about it."

"Well, what's the verdict?"

"The best candidate has been selected. Sorry, you can try again," the principal said and rose from his seat to signal the end of their conversation.

Rao did not accept the proffered hand and left the office with his head down and his teeth clenched behind his pressed down lips. Losing his appetite for lunch, he went upstairs to Clem's office, knocked gently and said, "Guess who the best candidate was?"

The paper Clem was reading jumped from his hands. "Don't tell me."

"Thought you should know. White!"

***

The multicultural evening was a huge success. The world was on stage. Spanish students dressed in native costumes improvised colourful tableaux with pulsating, syncopated rhythms and spirited background music; students from the West Indies performed high-octane dances with energetic songs and animated melodies; a group of East Indians told the poignant story, in a dance drama, of a master and his servant girl whom he loves but can't marry, to the rising and falling thump-thumps on the tabla drums; the Polish and Ukrainian dancers dazzled the audience with varieties of polkas intertwined with high-kicking and somersaults. Prior to the show, parents and students dined from a buffet table filled with sumptuous dishes of international cuisine—curried goat, carotas, samosas, rotis, tandoori chicken, goulash, beef fajitas, akee, kuskus, lentil dal, pulao, lasagna, and other dishes with exotic names, not to mention the traditional fare of salads, fruits and cakes—lovingly prepared by the home-ec students with some help from home.

Rao stood in the foyer of the auditorium and, beaming with obvious pride and satisfaction, his teeth gleaming, the corners of his mouth showing strains of perpetual smiling to which he was unaccustomed, he shook hands and accepted congratulations from parents, teachers, and students as they departed into the October night.

"Well done, Rao," said the principal, "a great show."

As the throng of parents thinned, Clem advanced towards his friend, the producer of the show, and patted him on the back of his camel wool jacket. "Excellent, just great," he gushed. "Remember this is the second step. Keep at it. You'll get there eventually."

That show gave a tremendous boost to Rao's ego—the residual kernel of one's self-esteem—and raised his leadership potential. He was acclaimed as the union rep for the second year. In May the business head let it be known that he was transferring to another school, and Rao saw his chance to make the move. However, he didn't have his specialist certificate. He was short of one credit—management accounting—in his core concentration. He pondered over this problem and began to search for a creative solution.

The yearend staff dinner was held at a restaurant in June. A special room was set aside for the party, which by 10 pm was humming with genial bonhomie and relaxed camaraderie. Some folks danced to the music of their own tapes, others clustered at the bar and, after having imbibed a few, began to swap hilarious stories of student ineptitude. Rao went up to the principal's table and whispered in his year. The principal, who had taken off his sports jacket and hung it on the back of his chair, rose to his feet and walked with Rao towards another table removed from the buzz.

"Sir, I've an interesting proposal for you," said Rao.

"Are you propositioning me?" the principal quipped and forced a laugh through his creased facial skin.

It was Rao's turn to laugh...*I'm glad he's in a good mood...*"I'm taking a summer course and—"

"Good for you," he said at once.

"I need the credit so I can take my business specialist next summer. But I need your help."

"My help? What way?"

"Well, I know our department head is leaving, and I want his job. I'm prepared to do his job starting in September, without the allowance. Next summer I'll get my specialist designation and will be ready for paid promotion. What do you say?"

"Interesting! But I can't give you an answer now. I'll have to think about it."

"That's all I ask, Sir, thank you."

***

Something about the season of autumn seemed to stimulate Rao, as if the rest of the seasons didn't really count. According to the Zodiac, he was a Libra, an even-tempered man who worked hard and took his responsibilities seriously. So after becoming an acting head of business and obtaining his specialist accreditation, he realized his goal and now after three years in the job, he wished to climb the corporate ladder higher. Outside his classroom the yellow leaves drifted in the October wind. Inside, Rao was holding a meeting with his department, consisting of three women and two men. Rao had called the meeting not to discuss issues of curriculum per se, but to address some concerns he had about the functioning of his department. He'd arranged the desks in a semicircle and he stood in front and paced as he talked. Approaching forty now, he still retained a profusion of thick black hair and his voice, clear as a bell, carried a musical lilt with a charm of its own.

"This won't take longer than it needs to be," he began, "but as your department head, I feel it's my duty to communicate with you freely and frankly about the concerns I have. Over the past couple of years, I've observed certain things. For example, a number of you are not coming to school on time; in fact, I've had to stand in for some of you because you arrived a few minutes late, after nine. This is against the school regulations, against the Education Act of Ontario, as you must know. Besides, it's not professional. I want you to be on time, be punctual."

The group merely stared at Rao with expressions of disbelief.

"Secondly, I've noticed a tendency among some of you to hit the road as soon as the bell rings. A number of students have come up to me after school and said they need help with the computers or their accounting assignments. We owe it to them. We're here to serve the students. So I ask you to be available after school. I appeal to your good sense, your Christian sense of duty and sacrifice. These are my concerns, and I hope you'll take them to heart, and make them your own. Are there any questions?" Pause. "Any comments?" Pause.

A stony silence greeted him. "If not, that's all. See you tomorrow."

Rao's little speech did not have its desired result. Nothing changed. By spring he felt as if he were slapped in the face. He'd applied for the VP's position and wanted an endorsement from the principal. He decided to find out.

"I've your application here on my desk, but before I sign it I've to tell you something."

Rao nodded and waited.

"There are serious complaints against you from the members of your department," said the principal, with a stern face matched by his cold blue gaze. "From what I hear, you've serious problems dealing with people. You've been preaching to them, I am told, about the virtues of punctuality, duty and sacrifice. The art of managing people involves adroitness, sensitivity and, yes, compassion, which qualities I am afraid, you do not seem to possess. To tell you the truth, I cannot recommend you under the circumstances."

For a week Rao smarted from the principal's rebuff...*I just don't get it. Instead of praising me for helping him do his job, the principal puts me down. Something is rotten in the inner sanctum of the school. Most outrageous! There must be a way out of this, there always is.*

Rao plotted his strategy and thought he'd run it by Clem, his mentor of sorts, who meanwhile had also been moving up, now head of social studies. It was the exam week in June. Seeing that Clem was not in his office, Rao walked to his classroom one floor up. He got an eerie feeling going through the deserted hallway, which only a week earlier had been bustling with students. He poked his head in the door that was left ajar and said "Hi."

The afternoon light from the window mirrored off Clem's receding forehead as he turned his face, beamed and said, "Hi, come in, I've something to tell you."

"Before you do that, let me tell you something," said Rao and stood in front of the teacher's desk in the left corner near the window. Clem put aside the papers he was grading, sheaves of foolscap essays, as Rao walked back and shut the door.

"I'm upset, I'm angry, and I won't take this lying down. You know that I applied for the VP's position?"

"I recall your telling me that."

"I am turned down flat. The principal won't recommend me." He narrated the chain of events leading up to his last meeting with the boss. "It's a clear case of discrimination, I'm telling you. I'm going to write a complaint to the superintendent. It's a clear case of unadulterated racism. I'll write to the board and the director, if I have to." He paced about, his slim figure taut as a prowling Bengal tiger's.

"Please sit down," said Clem. "Let me give you a piece of advice. Remember I am on your side. I want you to succeed. And you will succeed."

"I don't feel like sitting."

"Okay." Pause. "Don't take that route. It will block your chances in the future. From what you've told me, it appears you didn't handle it well, I mean your approach to your fellow teachers. It smacks of a superior attitude, and I suggest you tone it down. Be one of the boys. Play golf with them or tennis. That's the way to succeed in this business. You've made it thus far, so don't blow it."

An incredulous look appeared on Rao's sulking face, a look that suggested he was being censured, not understood...*I hear that patronizing tone again. Be a good boy, don't rock the boat.*

"I believed you were on my side, but no, you're all the same. You want to fatten yourself up and throw the crumbs at Lazarus like me. That's how you expiate your sins. You're nothing but a self-centered, self-promoter who knows on which side your bread is buttered, and with a mind on the main chance. Don't I know your kind? You wouldn't advise me like that if you were in my place."

Clem shook his head several times. He grabbed a few sheets of foolscap and pretended to read, as if giving his friend time to cool off. Then he told him, "But, Rao, I am not in your place." His blue eyes were as clear as they had been on the night of the dinner five years ago.

"What do you mean?"

"I've been promoted to VP—I'll be transferring to another school in September. That's what I wanted to tell you when you came in."

"You never told me that! You never told me you'd applied for the job."

"It's been a busy semester. And I wanted to keep it quiet until I found out for sure. I got the news only yesterday."

"Well, that explains it. He's not going to recommend two people from the same school in the same year."

"I'm sorry," said Clem and stood up. "I've a meeting with the boss in two minutes."

Quickly, like a cat confused by sudden light, Rao pivoted and headed towards the door. "Don't do what I wouldn't do," he heard Clem say. Rao paused at the door, straining with emotion to get the words out. "I got to do what I got to do."

Then he strode out through the forsaken corridor with its wall-length, dark and bruised lockers stripped of their vanities, his heroic heart determined to expose what he perceived to be a transparent case of racial prejudice.

Thoughts Never Die
by Bianca Lakoseljac

Getting up at four in the morning was not something Jennifer was accustomed to. The four hour bus ride from North Bay to Barrie, and then the forty-minute one to Wyevale, combined with delays had resulted in a lengthy road trip that had taken its toll on her. Peering through the haze of the summer heat, down the winding dirt road that seemed to stretch into infinity, she wished she had followed her husband Ron's advice and waited for Wyevale's only taxicab instead of choosing to walk. She thought the walk would do her good, give her time to think, to think of what to say. But now, the old farmstead seemed much farther than she remembered.

Quite a few years had passed since she'd been there, years of silence.

She sat on a boulder at the side of the road, dropping her overnight bag on a dry patch of weeds. The rectangular bulge in the right pocket of her thin, cotton shorts reminded her she needed to compose a greeting of some kind, an explanation. Would it be necessary? Perhaps, perhaps not.

Instinctively, she placed her hand in her pocket fingering the bundled sheets of paper. Seven pages, all folded tightly into a rectangle the size of a cigarette pack. Since coming across this letter again a few weeks ago, she had not been able to stop thinking about it. Not that she had ever completely forgotten it. It was always in the back of her mind, where she had pushed it, far in the back.

Keeping the letter tightly folded helped her keep its contents at bay, at the periphery of her thoughts. But now, as she slowly unfolded the well-thumbed pages, once more its presence regained the centre stage of her mind. Again, a sense of unease surfaced within her as she glanced at the inconsistent handwriting, some letters leaping forward and some reclining backward, retracted words scratched over until the original word was undetectable. And yet once more she was drawn into it. Lowering the brim of her Tilley hat over her forehead, she began reading:

"Hello Jen!

Why now, you ask? After all this time?

Because I have never stopped caring.

Because I have never given up.

Because I have never forgotten.

Recently, I went to Toronto for a doctor's appointment and decided to go for a stroll in High Park, my favourite, but then you know that. Remember us taking the kids to the little zoo down the hill, just down from the restaurant?

Well, I parked at the restaurant and walked south towards the arbour with hanging baskets, along the walkway between the two rows of purple barberry hedges, past the water fountains, and just a little farther down the hill. There is a bench I liked to sit on, way back when we all lived in that area. It has an incredible view of Grenadier Pond. On a sunny day, looking through the dappled shade of the old oaks, across the rolling greenness of the lawn, you can see the water sparkle.

You and I had sat on that bench once or twice, but you probably don't remember. As I said, I've sat there many times. Strangely, I've never noticed the inscription on it. And there it was:

Of memory, images, and precious
Thoughts that shall not die.

It was in memory of a loved one, Claire. I wondered who Claire was. What were her memories, her precious thoughts? I wondered if they were still alive.

And then I thought how precious life is. I thought of all the people I loved and you were there, as real as life itself.

I thought of our talks, our long walks, of our little children and their sweet little faces at various stages of their childhood—sweet toothless smiles etched forever in my memory.

Have you forgotten the sweet little faces of our children?

I have not. Only an old friend can have those memories.

I am sorry that you had a health scare. I hope all is well now. I also had a health scare about the same time.

Strange, that we should not be able to share and offer support. That's the problem with letters. You can only hear one side.

I can see that you're hurt. I understand. I am also hurt.

That evening on the phone, I *was* emotional. It seemed that you didn't understand the reason. I suppose we received mixed messages.

I had just lost my mother and was hurting badly. I was also very sad that after I called your house and told Ron that I'd lost my mother, you never called me back.

No phone call. No card. Nothing.

That really hurt.

And no note whatsoever from a person who writes cards and letters because she enjoys writing letters—on a bus, train, or wherever—letters I had welcomed.

I don't know if you realize what shape I was in that evening.

I was crying—and you hung up on me.

What would you have done if you had just lost your mother and I hung up on you—and while you were crying?

I could have never done that.

And instead of calling me back to resolve the misunderstanding, you began sending me a flurry of your "cute" notes. You kept asking me why I was not replying to you. As you recall, in the past I never had replied to your notes. I only write letters when I have to—and then they turn into a novel, but that's beside the point. You said you enjoyed writing and did not expect a reply. But this time you insisted. I was in mourning, and you kept insisting that I reply to notes written on pretty stationery with flowers and cats, notes about you and your interests, notes that trivialized my pain. Now that some time has passed, I can give you a few reasons why I had not replied.

The first note you sent me you talked about your wonderful relationship with your mother.

As you know, I was not as fortunate as you to have the same closeness with my mother. I failed at that. And since she was gone, it was too late.

51

It became clear to me that your writing was intended for you, not me; that you had little concern for your reader—me.

The second note was similar. You used the words, "I acknowledge your pain..."

Friends share. Friends cry together, call each other to see how the other is doing. Friends do not simply *acknowledge* the other's pain.

As the cliché goes, "It's easy to be friends in good times."

It is the bad times that bring true friendships to life.

I know I am emotional. I know my life is turbulent.

Perhaps I make it that way or perhaps that is the path God chose for me.

But I also care about you and need to know that a friend whom I love as if she were my sister cares about me.

I did not reply for I was sad and hurt. I also realized that your letters deepened my sadness and my loss.

Please do not misunderstand—not for a moment do I think I am perfect.

I have many faults and I have made many mistakes.

I am just as imperfect as anybody—just like you.

Besides, I did reply to one of your letters. Don't you remember? The one where you said you'd listen. So I replied, asking you not to treat me like your sounding board. I said I did not wish to be your pen pal and asked you to call me. But you simply wrote another letter.

Just to jog your memory, let me give you two reasons I do not wish to be your pen pal. First, do you remember your former pen pal, your childhood friend who stopped writing after she visited you?

I now know why.

The evening she came to visit you, remember? You told me you had a nice dinner and a wonderful conversation, and then it was bedtime for your kids. She had offered to wait until your kids were asleep—she had not seen you for many years and had traveled a long way—

but you thought it inconvenient to your family. So you asked her to leave.

To her you were a friend. To you she was just a pen pal. She realized that.

And here is my second reason: your way of keeping in touch is to write letters and mine is to phone. But lately, each time I phoned you, you had no interest in what I had to say.

I remember calling you after my visit to Europe, wanting to tell you about my family's experiences. You blatantly refused to hear me. I insisted. You said you weren't interested in my trip and wanted to tell me about your gardening projects. So I listened...for almost an hour...hoping you would eventually ask me about my trip. And you never did.

But the next day, you wrote me a detailed letter, forgetting how unkind you were. I realized I was simply a sounding board to you; that the letters provided you with the one-way communication you desired—enabled you to say what you wanted without the bother of listening to the other person.

Turning a friend into merely a pen pal is hurtful and dehumanizing.

Pen pals can be happy with each other if both are willing. I am not willing to be anyone's pen pal. I consider that type of relationship a waste of time and effort. In fact, more than that—but better left unsaid.

I realize that you know all of this. That is why I thought you would see what the problem is and remedy it. I thought that eventually you would phone me.

You and I became friends by talking, laughing, having lunches together, enjoying long walks—by sharing our lives. Letters are fine when they enhance personal communication. But once they replace it, they become meaningless.

Too many things are left unexplained, misunderstood—as you can see.

Too many impersonal, wasted, even hurtful words denying the opportunity for explanation.

My suggestion is: let's have a family reunion, get everybody together—our kids, their boyfriends, girlfriends, everyone.

Let's talk. Not about our failings but about us, family, life.

Love,
Your sister in spirit, Edwina

p.s.

Please do not write. Call me. Or come and visit.

If you can't decide what to do, please follow your heart.

And remember, that you or I can make new friends, but neither of us can ever make old friends.

Love,
Edwina"

Jennifer recalled replying to this letter and receiving it back, unopened. She wrote a few more times, but there was no reply. So she gave up, deciding that the friendship was over. A few weeks back as she was cleaning her dresser drawer, she came upon this same letter she thought she had thrown away some time ago. And then the dreams began, night after night, memories melding into dreams, dreams into memories.

One night it was Jennifer holding Edwina's train in front of the altar at Saint Joan of Arc on Bloor Street in Toronto. Everything was just like on the wedding day. Michael and Ron stood rigidly in their black tuxes and pleated white shirts. Suddenly, Edwina's white gown burst in flames as she floated up and up, vanishing into the vaulted ceiling. All Jennifer could see were the licking flames reflected in the mosaic of blues and greens, yellows and purples of the stained glass windows closing the gap above.

"This is ludicrous," Jennifer uttered out loud, as she got up from the boulder and picked up her bag.

Shaking off the large yellow ants crawling on the bag, she realized she had dropped it on an anthill. "Hope they're not fire ants," she mumbled to herself. "Solzhenitsyn's fire ants, as Edwina called them."

She stared into the anthill, at the innumerable little creatures scurrying around, and then remembered another Edwina-dream. The fire-ant-Edwina-dream. Edwina often quoted Aleksandr Solzhenitsyn's comments where he compared his choice to return to the Soviet Union to the fire ants' return into their nest in a burning log. In this dream, Edwina was a fire ant, returning to her apparent home in a burning tree trunk. Jennifer had screamed at Edwina to stop. She had even stuck her hand into the flames trying to grab the little Edwina-ant out of the fire. As she woke up, Jennifer swore she could still feel the fire burning her hand. She even checked for the burn, puzzled she found none. The dreams were so vivid, they haunted her waking hours.

"I should be turning back," Jennifer muttered, as she resumed her slow walk towards the farm, into the mirage of heat, crickets scattering about her feet like popcorn. She smiled to herself: *Popcorn. Yes, your cottage.* This was not a dream. This was a memory.

We had put on your mismatched oven mitts, Jennifer began her mental chat with Edwina, and held a long iron handle of that funny contraption over the fire. We shook it, popcorn flying out all around us, our children's laughter jingling against the gurgling of the creek, their voices skipping with the stream, over the makeshift waterfall of rocks Michael and Ron had built earlier in the day. Sitting on a log suspended over two tree stumps, our husbands sipped their beer, their feet extended towards the stones guarding the fire. The kids made smores—squishing the sandwiched Graham Wafer cookies, roasted marshmallows and melted chocolate dripping between their fingers, doing Hanz and Franz from stand-up comedy and laughing, laughing, their chocolate-smudged faces glistening in the glowing flames.

"I think I know the answer," you whispered: "It's about love and memories and precious thoughts."

I knew what you meant. How could I not? You sought the meaning of life in all the things most people took for granted: in the smell of the earth between the patches of the melting snow in early spring; in the flowers that bloomed in your garden, from snowdrops and tulips to fragrant pinks, summer phlox and roses, and mums scorched by early frost; in white butterflies your Kitty

shook with her paw out of the silver-leaf dogwood; in blue jays
and red cardinals and the resident doves in your backyard; in
rain and thunder and sunshine and the reflection of the
shimmering lake; and the sunsets...especially the sunsets. But
most of all you were awed by the miracle of raising children and
having a family. So I knew what you meant.

"And here I am now, coming to visit you Edwina,
unannounced, simply because I can't get you out of my
thoughts," Jennifer mumbled.

She decided that showing up in person would be easier
than telephoning. Didn't Edwina always say that she valued
personal chitchats above all other means of keeping in touch?
...And that, over herbal tea and homemade cookies. So Jennifer
had baked a batch of oatmeal-walnut with brown sugar, Edwina's
favourite, and brought them along. Besides, coming to visit
seemed the only way. What would one say over the phone after
all this time?

Carefully, she folded the letter along the old creases until
it was again the size of a cigarette pack and stuffed it back in her
pocket. She slung her bag over her shoulder and resumed her
slow trek under the blazing afternoon sun. Finally, she made the
bend and was standing on the hill under the frayed shade of the
towering, wind-beaten white pine. This was the landmark where
the old farmstead magically appeared in full view—as if out of
nowhere, around the bend and down the hill, now only a few
hundred yards away.

Jennifer thought it strange that several cars were parked
on the lawn in front of the house. Edwina and Michael avoided
large gatherings. Was there an occasion? It wasn't anyone's
birthday, at least not that she recalled.

And then the familiar old Buick was weaving its way
towards her. It stopped beside her.

"Michael? Is that you?" She uttered, barely recognizing
this aged figure of the Michael she knew.

"Jen," he answered flatly, unsurprised, as if expecting to
see her.

Michael reached into his pocket. "She left this for you.
She carried it in her purse God knows for how long." He pulled
out a rectangular bundle of paper folded over until it was the size
of a cigarette pack. He unfolded it slowly, revealing a tattered
envelope addressed to Jennifer. "She thought that some day

56

she'd send it to you. A week ago she gave it to me and said to mail it after she... Strange, this morning just before the funeral, I stuffed this letter in my pocket. Somehow, it made me feel closer to her. Now, I was on my way to the mailbox... And here you are..."

"Before the funeral? Did you say...?"

"Didn't you know? Edwina passed away three days ago. We buried her this morning... I thought that's why you're here... Didn't you get the call? I thought you were on the list I gave to... But let's go down to the house," Michael continued. "You must be exhausted. Let's have some of Edwina's favourite cookies—she'd like that. I have at least a dozen versions of her oatmeal-walnut-with-brown-sugar recipe. Just about every woman in Wyevale has brought a batch..."

Jennifer stared blankly at the tattered envelope with her own name on it, her eyes glazed, *seeing* through the dappled shade of the old oaks, across the rolling greenness of the lawn, seeing the water sparkle... "Thoughts never die..." she whispered, "Thoughts never die..."

Sweet Water
by Allyson Latta

Hiro came for her at seven, punctual as always, his bike rumbling up to her *manshion* and honking cheekily three times. She was washing up from her dinner when she heard, and ran in her bare feet over the *tatami* mats. Opening her door, she leaned over the rail of her second-floor apartment's useless little balcony – too narrow to sit on, it was mostly for hanging clothes to dry and futons to air. She waved with one hand, pushing her fair hair out of her eyes with the other.

"Ready?" he called up.

Anna thought he looked good, better than good, in his jeans and navy T-shirt. He was also wearing a huge grin today. His moods were a bit unpredictable, part of his charm, but he could be more fun than anyone she'd ever met. Once, for a costume party, she's dressed as Anne of Green Gables and he'd surprised her by donning green and painting his handsome face purple, sporting a green construction-paper crown on his head. *What are you supposed to be? An eggplant, can't you tell?*

"You're not going to give me a hint where we're going?"

"*Ie*, it's a surprise."

"I'm not sure going for a bike ride in rainy season is such a smart idea." She eyed the mountains in the distance, the grey of the early evening sky.

"When are you going to learn to trust me? But, bring an umbrella." That grin again.

Grabbing her fold-up umbrella and knapsack and slipping on a light jacket, she headed out, the steel door of her apartment clanging and echoing in the stairwell as she descended. Like a prison gate, she thought, not that she ever felt held here; she had more freedom than she ever could have imagined. Still, that jarring sound always sent her running down the stairs and out.

Astride the Suzuki, Hiro, wearing a blue helmet, handed her a red one with a yellow strip. His smiling eyes regarded her – more thoughtfully than usual? – as she strapped it on. Then she climbed on behind him and moulded her body to his, legs in jeans pressed to his hips, breasts to his back. It was a comfortable fit.

"Are we going to a *karaoke* box?" she asked, knowing full well how stubborn he was. If he wasn't ready to tell her, he wouldn't.

"You *gaijin*," he muttered, revving the bike and starting off. "So impatient." He had to raise his voice above the growl of the engine. "You just have to wait and see!"

They were probably off to a party somewhere, but with Hiro, one never knew. He had a playfulness that she was drawn to, had been since the beginning. Hiro was head teacher at the small ESL school called Way (the name of which made about as much sense as any Japlish place name) where she taught. His English was excellent because he'd studied for two years in L.A. He'd even had an American girlfriend, one he'd kept in touch with for some time after returning to Japan, though the relationship had petered out. Sandra eventually tired of pining for him.

When Anna thought about Sandra, that mystery woman, she felt a stab of jealousy, though she had no right. She had no hold on Hiro. He was her friend. Though, there had been times when she thought he might be more, could be more. Men were confusing, whatever their country of origin. At twenty-four she hadn't yet figured them out, though she hadn't entirely given up hope that she might.

As he drove, Anna peered over his shoulder, watching the play of muscles in his forearms as he gripped the handlebars. They had slept together once, months ago. Had come home from a party, full of Sapporo and good humour, their senses and curiosity alive. He'd kissed her just inside her clanging steel door, the taste of his mouth yeasty-salty from beer and *edamame*, and in moments they'd been inside, on the futon, clothes flying. He was a good lover, but oh, it was the softness of his skin that she remembered. Soft as a child's. Even the soles of his feet, always protected, never barefoot except on *tatami*. She'd asked him how to say it in Japanese. *Yawarakai hada*, he told her. Soft skin.

One night of passion hadn't changed anything between them. She wasn't sure why women assumed, time and again, that sex would. A few days of awkwardness followed; they didn't speak of it. Before long they were back to their usual banter, spending much of their free time together. He'd kissed her twice since then, both times when they had been drinking. Both times she'd kissed him back, and she would sleep with him again, she thought, though he hadn't asked. She thought she could imagine a life with him, here. She could also imagine one without him, back home – though her mental picture of home was growing increasingly blurry around the edges. Perhaps she didn't know what she wanted any more than he did.

Wind teasing their faces, they wound their way through the city, beyond the wider streets where the yellow streetcar grumbled and clacked and where the restaurants and bars with their colourful neon signs beckoned, to the outskirts that were lined with gawdy *pachinko* parlours full of hopeful gamblers, and where narrow, winding streets curved off into a maze of tiny homes with clay-tile roofs. Once in a while he reached down and squeezed her thigh.

He was definitely driving too fast, but Anna loved the speed, the feel of breaking free of the city. Soon they were racing along country roads among glistening, spring-water-laden rice paddies, catching a glimpse here of a farmer in a straw hat, there of a woman in what looked like a giant baby bonnet. Hiro was taking them northeast, toward ancient Mount Aso, watchful in the distance.

"*Inaka, desu ne?*" Country, isn't it. She said it above the engine noise, thinking to amuse him with her meagre Japanese. In the side mirror, she saw him smile. Just where *was* he taking her?

It was growing dark when she spotted a flash of orange ahead, and realized as they approached that it was a torch being waved by an elderly Japanese man wearing white gloves, like the taxi drivers in town. He gestured toward a crude parking lot, a field really. Hiro pulled the bike to a stop and they hopped off.

She turned slowly, glancing around. He had brought her to the middle of nowhere, it seemed. The air felt warm and moist. Faintly, in the distance, she heard gurgling water. A hot spring? Then, staticky Japanese music, badly amplified, as if wafting from the fields themselves. The rich smell of *shoyu*-flavoured snacks. But this couldn't be a festival, it was too subdued.

"Let's go," said Hiro, adding, "This is Kyokushi," as if that explained all.

The darkness confused her and she didn't know what lay ahead, so she took the hand he offered. As he pulled her along, the water's chortling grew more vivid and she noticed a string of torches in the distance, set in the ground and spaced out to provide illumination, but not too much of it. She was very aware of him, his height only a few inches more than hers, his shoulders broad. She liked Hiro's body, an athlete's body – he'd been one in high school and still trained – taut and smooth. He'd tried to get her to run with him, but the one time they'd done so, up and around Kumamoto Castle, he'd left her doubled over and panting.

They made their way past a rough-hewn concession tent plunked incongruously in a field, a vender doling out food, and the aroma lured her even though she'd just eaten. The music she'd heard was emanating from the booth as well, haunting *shamisen*, man-made, not nature-spun after all. As the tinny strains receded behind them, Anna noticed shadowy movement ahead and to her right. People, some of them obviously children, shuffling along and whispering occasionally in the faint light of torches along a path by what was clearly the river.

"Be careful where you walk," Hiro said, indicating a concrete walkway that traced the river's edge.

Anna was used to the reverence with which the Japanese viewed nature, but there was something eerie about this group – how many were out here? she couldn't tell – moving quietly, purposefully along. She thought fleetingly of lemmings, yet couldn't resist the pull herself.

"Only in Japan," she said. When Hiro found one of her Canadianisms funny, he'd say, in the same incredulous tone, *Only in Canada*. He couldn't believe they made such an effort not to slurp their noodles.

What he said now was "Patience."

And then, as they rounded a graceful curve in the river, she stopped abruptly, for before her, strung across the water and against a dark backdrop of tall pines, was a brilliant tapestry of flickering, pale yellow lights. Thousands upon thousands of them. She blinked and tried to focus on one light, follow it, then another, but each disappeared as if defying such limitation. Above, the sky was overcast and empty-looking. Heaven seemed to have rained all its stars down upon this place.

"What—?"

"*Hotaru*," he said. "This is *hotaru-gari*. Firefly viewing." He nudged her arm. "A good surprise?"

Her amazement must have shown in her face. She heard him chuckle. "Oh yes. *Yes,*" she breathed.

Murmurs floated about her. *Segoi.* Wonderful. *Kirei.* Beautiful. And then Hiro's voice: "They say they only live where the water is sweet and pure. They started coming here five years ago – no one knows why exactly." He paused. "As it becomes more popular, I'm sure, the river will be lined with *yakitoriya.*"

"There are ... so many." It seemed impossible to attribute such ethereal beauty to lowly bugs and their chemical reactions.

"Maybe thirty thousand, I've heard," he said.

"As if anyone could count fireflies. Talk about Sisyphean."

"Si-sy-phe-an." He prounced it stiltedly. "I'll need to look it up."

Anna was already moving forward, awestruck by the display of lights, the whole constant but the pattern endlessly shifting. She'd only ever seen fireflies at a friend's cottage in the Kawarthas, and there they had been sparser, teasing the corners of her eyes. Here the astonishing ensemble scintillated as if performing for their audience, clusters gracefully separating and then coalescing. Individually, they were elusive, taunting; together they mesmerized.

"A Sisyphean task," she said absently, not taking her eyes off the spectacle, "is one that's endless. Sisyphus was a Greek punished for his sins – he had to roll a rock up a hill. Forever."

"Hmm, I'll have to teach that one to my students."

She pulled her eyes away from the *hotaru* and looked at him. "Oh yes, a very handy phrase for beginners. 'Hello, how are you. My name is Yoshiko and my task is Sisyphean.'"

He took her hand again and his felt warm. The moment to her seemed perfect. Hiro. The night, the *hotaru.* She rarely thought about Canada these days, it seemed so far away. Her undergrad behind her. Mom and Dad divorced; her older sister married and settled down to a suburban existence. Here she had a job she loved, respect as a teacher, and friends, mostly Japanese teachers at Way. And the adventure of Japan, with surprises around every corner – every curve in the river.

His lips close to her ear, voice low, Hiro started singing:
Ho, ho, hotaru koi, atchi no mizu wa nigai zo,
kotchi no mizu wa amai zo;
ho, ho, hotaru koi, ho, ho, yama michi koi.

Anna shivered at the heat of his breath near her nape. He'd once told her that Japanese men find women's napes one of the sexiest parts of their body. Ah, Hiro. She recognized a few words: *hotaru* ... firefly ... *mizu* ... water ... *amai* ... sweet ... *yama* ... mountain. Though she loved the rhythm of the language, the full sense sometimes escaped her.

"What does it mean?"

"It's a child's song. I forget all the words. It begins—" He thought for a moment. *"Ho, firefly, come, there's some water that's bitter to taste. Come, here's some water that's sweet to your taste. Come, up this mountain path ..."*

"Teach it to me?"

"Of course." He cleared his throat. "But later. Not here, not right now," he said, gesturing as a stream of dark bodies approached and flowed around them, as if she and he were logs jammed in the riverbed.

Standing still made her uncomfortable. She preferred movement, always.

"Promise?" she said.

"Yes, I'll teach it to you ..."

A beat of silence. His tone had turned serious.

"... before I go."

An emphasis on the word *go* that she didn't like. "Go? Where?"

"I've been meaning to tell you, Anna. Trying to decide *how* to tell you."

She waited. Occasional brighter flares from cameras – observers trying to capture the uncontainable – blended into this night of lights. Dark figures formed a procession that wound out of view. She suddenly realized that she did, and yet didn't want to follow the path to its end.

"I'm moving back," he said finally. "To L.A."

She was aware that she would sound petulant but couldn't help herself. "Sandra?"

"No, no, that's over. Has been for a long time. But L.A. I know."

How ironic, after Sandra's years of waiting. "When?"

"Soon. Before summer. I'm going to do my M.A. in Linguistics. There are some courses I want to take first. I need to settle in."

The thought crashed in: *You can't go.* It was quickly followed by guilt. What she meant was *You can't go before me.*

"You'll be leaving soon too," he said, having read her mind. "You know you will. Back to Canada."

She felt panic rising. As if his words had banished her. She didn't even like to think about leaving this place. Couldn't. She had time left on her contract, and even then, perhaps she would not go.

Before she could answer, he said, huskily, "Anna-*chan*, walk with me. I brought you to see the fireflies." He took her hand again, and this time the feel of it as they strolled made her chest hurt. "Did you know," he said, "that *hotaru-zoku* is what we call people who smoke outside their buildings at night, because from inside, the cigarette ends look like fireflies?"

He knew her, knew that like him she loved language, even the trivia. It was only one of the things they shared. *Yawarakai hada.* Soft skin. *Atchi no mizu wa nigai zo.* There's some water that's bitter to taste....

"Maybe I just won't," she said, ignoring what he'd said.

"Won't what?"

"Leave. I like it here – it feels like home now."

"I know that's how it seems, but you won't stay. It's not your life." He paused. "If I stayed, you would leave *me* some day." She thought she heard pain there – or did she just need to believe that? None of this made sense. He had to leave his country, yet he was so sure she would return to hers? They were both suspended. "What if I told you I love you?" It was out before she could stop it, and she felt herself flush, realizing the Japanese around them certainly would understand those three little words.

"I love you too," he said without hesitation, though in a whisper.

Her throat was tight and wouldn't let her swallow.

He began again. "Sometimes I think you are the only one here who understands me, but ..."

So there it was. But.

"Well, maybe I don't." Anna stopped walking and turned away from him, toward the *hotaru*. She felt as if she were no longer watching the fireflies but among them, one of them, her bioluminescence fading. And which one was he – there and then not there, lighting up and then disappearing, leaving her dizzy?

She stretched out her hand toward the fireflies. Let it drop, empty.

A loud splash and then churning of water. Urgent Japanese, sharp admonishments, followed by relieved laughter. Murmurs and titters rippling along the line. She could make out the shadows of people hoisting someone from the river, dripping, a giggling child, perhaps six or seven years old from the look of him. Had he fallen, or did he too ache to touch the magical lights? The distraction broke the tension between them.

"Did you know," Hiro said as they passed the knot of onlookers near the boy and rounded another bend in the river, "that fireflies have been used as a symbol ... what's the word? A metaphor? For love, passionate love. There was a Japanese poet in the eighth century ... I've forgotten his name."

"You just looked that up," she said accusingly.

"True. I knew you'd ask me some of your endless questions."

She moved closer so that his face was inches from hers, too-bright in the glow of a nearby torch. "'Passionate love'? Just what are you trying to do to me here?"

"Anna-*chan*, I'm sorry. I was just ..."

"I know."

"... trying to change the subject."

"Not very well."

They both laughed, but at that moment she realized what they were, these *hotaru*. A goodbye. "Tell me something else," she said quickly. She no longer held his hand, feared she would seem to be clinging.

"About *hotaru*? Well, some Japanese believe they are the souls of soldiers who have died in war."

"The souls of soldiers *and* the embodiment of passionate love? Only in Japan," she said, shaking her head.

"Only in Japan," he repeated. "But love and war ... they are two sides of the same koka." He grimaced. "Okay, that was bad."

"Yes, it was. Anyway, I'd rather think the lights were the souls of lovers—" Her voice caught and gave her away. *Shit.*

"Anna-*chan*, I—"

"I'm okay."

She wasn't sure, but she thought that perhaps in time she would be.

As Anna moved forward she felt him following close, and she drew in a deep breath, then exhaled, forcing her sadness away, beyond the gurgling river and the silhouetted pines and the thousands of tiny, flickering lights.

She felt the first cool drop on her cheek, another on her arm, and then before she could even pull her umbrella from her pack, the deluge began and around her dozens of umbrellas shot up and opened like the wings of giant birds taking flight, blocking out the *hotaru*. They were still there, though, she felt sure, darting between raindrops, holding their secret light inside them, just out of reach above that pure flowing river, that sweet water.

A noisy, jostling exodus began, everyone making for the concession tent, the only shelter. Hiro was already drenched, grinning once again and holding his arms out like a suppliant.

Anna fumbled with slippery hands to open her own umbrella, but gave up. "Come on," she said to him, raising her voice over the beating rain. "Let's run."

A Star for the Colonel
by George Bernstein

In foggy cold dawn drizzle, Zulu patrol crept up to Tango sector, a low hill, near Ortona, on the Adriatic side of mid-Italy. Sergeant McGirr scooted around the hill as we cocked our Stens to cover him. He raised his arm when a loud clatter echoed through the fog. We all hit the ground belly first as machine gun fire rattled at us from every direction. The Sergeant heaved a grenade and we heaved a few more, then opened up with the Stens. Our Sherman battle tank loomed out of the fog and the fire-fight was over.

While collecting and disarming enemy weapons, I accidentally dropped one out of a pile I held in my arms. A bloodied corpse pulled it towards him. I watched his fingers tighten around the trigger of his Schmeisser machine pistol. The shots catching me in the belly.

Stretcher-bearers carried me to an Advanced Sspitote Casualty Post.

A medic started plasma in my arm, gave me a shot of morphine, unstuck my lips and pushed a lit cigarette between them. The morphine started to work in a few minutes and I thought I could hear angel music.

They loaded me into a half-track. We jostled a mile or so to a Field Dressing Station.

The medics put me just inside the tent entrance. I saw casualties lying there, in blood soaked uniforms. Plasma dripped slowly into the arms of fellows covered with sheets. Nurses moved through the maze of stretchers and cots and cast surreal shadows on the dimly lit tent walls, flapping in the rainy gusts. A nurse hurried to me. She cut away part of my uniform and inspected my wound in the beam of a flashlight held by a medic. She turned as she heard the softly spoken curses of a medic covering the soldier to my right with a tattered sheet. A grey haired chaplain spoke softly to a soldier opposite me.

A haggard medical officer shuffled to my stretcher. He felt my pulse, checked my eyes with a pocket light, and uncovered my wounds. Turning to his nurse and thinking I was too far gone to hear, said, "This lad has bought it." Noting the silver star of David chained to my dog tags (and worn against regulations) added, "Try and contact a Rabbi Chaplain if you can."

"No!" I murmured. Miserable was I. I could scarcely breathe.

I found out later that my three buddies, having overheard the doctor, tried to find a Chaplain. Failing in this, they commandeered a jeep and actually kidnapped a Divisional Rabbi Chaplain who was a full Colonel.

Forehead wrinkled with my pain, Colonel Wallenburg asked me to recite with him, the confession. He spoke the Hebrew words - words that have echoed through the centuries from Masada to Auschwitz to Entebbe: "Adoshem Melech, Adoshem Moloch....L'ulomV'ed."

At this , I panicked.

"Rabbi, I'm positive I'm not dying. I really don't feel that bad."

"My son, The Lord, in His compassion, blessed be His name, has lessened your pain."

"Please sir! May I be examined by another doctor. If he thinks I'm dying, I promise I'll go out like a man."

The Colonel soon returned with Col. Chamberlain Weber. He examined me, then chatted briefly with the junior medical officer by his side. Turning to Rabbi Wallenburg he said "Colonel, we're transferring this soldier to our Unit Field Hospital for immediate surgery. And Colonel, with help from your Commander-in-Chief he'll likely survive."

The medic hooked up another bottle of plasma to my I.V. line and gave me another jolt of morphine. Then the stretcher-bearers loaded me on to a sputtering jeep. My buddy, Big Bill Zebreski looked approvingly at the vehicle and gave me a sly wink. Jim Cohen and Joe Bradley gave me the thumbs-up sign. The outside fog seemed to be working into me and I had difficulty seeing.

The jeep roared and lurched through the mud, until we arrived in the village of Santa Caterina.

The 1st Canadian Corps Field Hospital was not the large tent affair I had envisioned but a converted old wine warehouse - Graziano e Fellini - Magazzino de Vino. I was left at an admitting station. The smell of ether and antiseptics prevailed. A nurse walked to my stretcher, adjusted my plasma line and checked my pulse and blood pressure. She smiled. "You're in reasonably good shape soldier. You'll be going to the operating area shortly."

A short time later, a wheezing old man supervised my transfer by two equally ancient chaps, who by their complexion were likely former employees of Graziano e Fellini. The old guy gave me, between wheezes, a rousing preoperative pep talk in Italian and then with surgical precision, rolled me into the operating area.

Two surgeons walked over to my cart. Each examined me, and went off to the side a few feet and spoke to each other. Then Dr. Hugh Mallory-Gibson told me my bowel had been nicked at several areas with 9 millimeter slugs. I would need two or three operations and would likely be able to leave the hospital in eight weeks. And then with a smile, "Nurse O'Riley - Lt. O'Riley is section chief of your ward."

It was difficult coming out of the anaesthetic. Nothing happened when I tried to move my arm or leg. Everything was in duplicate or triplicate - or like looking through ground glass.

In a few days, I was functioning reasonably well. Lt. O'Riley silently changed my dressings. I grunted and groaned more than necessary. She smiled, "When you fellows make all that noise, it's a sign you are getting better."

Next evening we talked. She was married to the skipper of the corvette, HMCS Swordfish.

She spoke about the elimination of the U-boat menace and the way the war was turning. She was to see her husband soon, as they were getting leave together and would meet in Naples.

I was disappointed about this skipper-intruder in my love life and turned to a game of checkers with my neighbour. He was a RCAF sergeant-navigator who required plastic surgery for facial burns. He was a very bad checkers player. He told me his game was bridge, which I knew nothing about; the usual stand-off between the Army and the Air Force.

Colonel Wallenburg visited me a few days later. The Levine tube was still in my stomach and poking out of my nose. The Colonel frowned and blinked when I gagged on the tube as I spoke.

"Just relax private and let me do the talking, okay? When they get that tube out of you in a few days, I won't be able to get a word in." He hoped that all of us could spend the next Hanukkah and Christmas at home in peace. I heard the shooting and saw the flashes in the sky that night. I wasn't unhappy about being in the hospital.

The next morning the Colonel peeked into our ward. "I asked Dr. Colson if you could come to chapel for prayers today. It's the Sabbath."

From that Sabbath on, I prayed with the Rabbi. He gave me his prayer book. It was worn and had the German translation of the Hebrew, rather than the English I was used to. My grandmother owned a prayer book like this one, having brought it with her when she left Germany. I mentioned this to the Rabbi. He seemed to look beyond me and beyond the ward. "My grandparents are still in Germany."

Rabbi Colonel Wallenburg was over six feet, with flaming red hair, likely in his mid-thirties. They said when he was alone at night in the chapel, he would stare out the window looking at the 105 millimeter flashes in the sky. Jane Galway, the surgical ward nurse, told me that whenever we had a large number of casualties he would talk with the wounded for days on end, and had to be ordered to get some sleep by his commanding officer. The Rabbi was popular with the other chaplains. Father Legault told the Colonel about the advantages of converting to Christianity - this over a bottle of Dewer's twelve year old Scotch. The Colonel said that if he got back to Toronto, with all the decorations George VI had conferred on him, his pulpit contract would be five times that of a Quebec parish priest. The Colonel indicated that it was all just a matter of economics. Father Legault took an extra slug of Scotch and asked the Colonel what was the best rabbinical seminary that the Father could enrol in. Then they both roared with laughter and walked out arm in arm.

In two more weeks, if things went right, I would be discharged from the hospital. This was the first Sabbath that the Rabbi was not in the chapel for prayers. I saw Father Legault, on several occasions, walking, lost in thought and with no cheerful greetings. I wasn't happy during those two weeks. I thought that the rumble of the 105's was getting to me.

It was time to return to my unit. I waited to say goodbye to Lt. O'Riley. The supervisor, Captain McEvoy, looked at the floor as she told me that Lt. O'Riley would be away for a few days as "Swordfish" struck a mine and went down with all hands. I asked about Colonel Wallenburg. She started to say something then turned and walked away.

A dour Scotch welcome from Sarge McGirr awaited me when I returned to B company; guard duty in the rain to get used to my scratchy uniform. Our brigade was well north of Ortona. There were some missing faces, I knew we must have taken a beating as we pushed north. I asked Bill Zebreski about the Rabbi but he turned away to clean his gun. Jim Cohen grabbed me and said in a voice I could barely hear, "Sorry, bad news. The Colonel was killed in action two weeks ago."

Many years have passed since I last saw the Rabbi Col David Ira Wallenburg, D.S.O., M.C. at the Field Hospital. Yet I often think of him.

As a surgeon, death is no stranger. Sometimes I see these spectres grinning at me from every corner of the operating area. Our philosophies are bankrupted when they try to explain or justify death.

Who prayed with my Rabbi as his soul ascended to his God?

TALE OF THE RED MONKEY
by M.E. Kowalski

Unlike the other clubs and bars in Hong Kong's Lan Kwai Fong bar district, The Red Monkey had never been described as "chic," "shi shi" or "to die for" in local nightlife magazines. Nor had it ever been mistaken for one of the more sophisticated watering holes in the area. It lacked the trendy décor, the fusion-cooking and beautiful people sipping expensive, multi-coloured cocktails. The Red Monkey was a place for those who were most comfortable with their buddies, a pint and a bowl of peanuts - a dimly lit pub whose walls housed a treasury of cheap posters depicting fox hunting, British soldiers in India and pipe-smoking dogs playing cards. Its mascot, a ragged, but fierce-looking chimpanzee that loomed out into the street, was a favourite of Rogers. He never passed up a chance to put his arm around some unsuspecting, Japanese tourist having her picture taken in front of it; usually striking a lecherous pose that would be noticed only when the photos were developed. In all, it was the perfect starting point for our nights out.

There had been five of us who had pal'd around in the service of Her Majesty's Government of Hong Kong: myself, Armitage, Rogers, Merton, and Crawford. We had joined up within months of each other in late 1979, young, eager and ready to take on the world. The four of us (the four *gweilo* as Crawford, the lone Asian, called us) had left home for Asia, spurred on by dreams inspired by Conrad, Maugham and Mason.

At the moment, however, I had our usual table at The Red Monkey all to myself. Across the street, an old, Chinese street-vendor was selling flashing, mobile phone face-plates. She looked very much like a mamasan from the Kit Kat Club, one of several bars from which Rogers had gotten us banned. That night the mamasan had seated us in the mezzanine. "Hello, what have we got here?" Merton had said looking down at an amorous couple in a mild state of undress. Rogers leaned over the railing, intending to drop some nuts onto them, but in so doing, leaned too far and fell over the tiny railing. A large indoor tree broke his fall before he landed onto the couple. The man turned out to be the spoiled son of one of Hong Kong's richest families which guaranteed that the ensuing melee of bodyguards, police and drunken ex-patriates would be front page news in the next edition of the South China Morning Post.

Rogers always seemed to be looking for the next adventure, whether it was his infamous leap to the Star Ferry as it left the docks – he missed, and spent two weeks in hospital recovering from the bacterial infection he received from the putrid harbour – or clambering through old WW II fortifications. One night he came to The Red Monkey with a newspaper clipping about an ex-pat gunned down in Tsim Sha Tsui. The ex-pat had been whipping down the street on his motorcycle, when he was shot to death by members of a triad. "Can you imagine?" Rogers had said. "Wind in your hair, a pretty girl clinging to your waist, and down you go - in a blaze of glory. What a way to go!"

"Actually, I can't," I said. "There is something very classy and civilized about dying in bed."

"So your wife can wake up next to your stiff, clammy body and have a heart attack?" Rogers said. "Or, better yet, so that no one finds your body for days until the superintendent wonders about the smell? No thanks." He waved his hand at me in a manner that suggested I was beyond help. "Now," he continued. "Who's up for a bungee jump? I found this perfect spot on the pedestrian bridge along The Peak."

Like all good things, our time in Hong Kong came to an abrupt, but not unexpected, end with the 1997 hand-over to China. Staying after the hand-over for us four *gweilo* was not an option - not in the government at least. The unwritten rule in the civil service was to replace all senior Caucasian faces with Chinese ones. The Hong Kong Government was to be a Chinese government in spirit and body. With the exception of Rogers who stayed in Hong Kong with Crawford, we went back to countries we hadn't lived in for a generation, to look for employers willing to hire 40 year-old ex-civil servants.

It was fitting that Crawford should stay on in the Hong Kong government. He could trace his Hong Kong roots back more than a century and his veins ran deep with a rich mixture of races; it gave him the appearance of a full-blooded Chinese. His superb language skills, UK private school education and what he called "the correct physical features," allowed him to remain in government, where he could quickly vault through a variety of positions left vacant by the exodus of Caucasian ex-patriots.

Rogers was an only child whose parents had long since died. "So, what the hell have I got to go back to?" he said. "I've lived the most important half of my life here." He took a quaff from his beer. "Besides," he joked, "Someone's got to look after Crawford. Unlike you other bastards, I feel a moral obligation to stay on here to watch over him. You know, white man's burden." Crawford gave Rogers a good-natured forearm to the shoulder coupled with a sharp "Fuck you, mate."

In the late Spring of 1997, we were sitting in The Red Monkey when Rogers hatched the idea of our reunion. We all agreed that it was a brilliant idea, but the conversation quickly veered onto more immediate matters; Merton's flight was leaving in the morning and mine was just a day after that, making this, our final night of debauchery. The reunion on the other hand, was years in the future; there was no need to take it seriously at that moment. The beer continued to flow and we staggered through every bar in Lan Kwai Fong, but Rogers' resolve to make the reunion a success did not lessen. In fact, the thought of a reunion seemed to make him uncharacteristically sentimental. At one point, he shoved the group of us against a wall. "Hold on, hold on," he slurred. "There's something I want to say." We stared back drunkenly. "I'm not usually this sappy, but, you bastards are the only family I've got – I'm really going to miss you guys." He herded us together for a drunken group-hug.

"Alright, alright, that's enough of your babbling," Merton said pushing Rogers aside. "I haven't had enough to drink to let your sweaty paws fondle my body, mate." We staggered onward, chalking up Rogers' strange behaviour to general drunkenness.

We finished that night back at The Red Monkey, where Rogers once more brought up the subject of the reunion. "We need a vow," he blurted out.

"A vow?" It was Armitage. "What the hell are you yammering about?"

"A vow! A goddamned vow," Rogers slammed his fist hard on the round oak table. "We need to make a solemn vow to reunite in Hong Kong, five years hence. Christmas, 2002."

We all looked at each other and then at Rogers.

I slowly raised my glass. "Sure," I said. "I'm in."

Rogers gave me a look of disgust. "Make the Goddamned vow," he said again. Then, as one, we shouted "Five years hence!" and raised our glasses together as if they were swords and we were a group of musketeers off to save the King.

Five years went by quicker than I could have imagined. During that time, I clawed along the fat, layer of middle–management of a large insurance company; Merton got married and had two kids; Armitage opened a small bookstore in Manchester and got engaged – twice.

So now, here I was.

Five years hence.

Christmas, 2002, in Hong Kong.

As scheduled.

Alone.

I quaffed the last of my third pint and absentmindedly let the empty glass slam down hard on the table. Around me, The Red Monkey steadily filled with homesick young Aussies and older, grey-haired white men with meek, Asian girlfriends. It was now forty-five minutes past our appointed meeting time. Where the hell were they? Was I the only fool to fly back? I looked at the four empty seats at the table. They looked forlorn and lonely in the dim bar lighting - like homely girls and geeky guys along the gym wall at a high school dance. They made me look all the more pathetic.

A Chinese girl walked into The Monkey, wearing a scowl and a short red blouse that displayed a sliver of cinnamon tummy above her low slung jeans. She shot a deadly stare at a guy in a nautical-looking blazer – a look that should have struck him dead. Catching her eyes, he quickly glanced down at his watch before slamming his drink to the bar and hurrying over to meet her. But she had already turned and left.

A voice spoke from behind me. "Doghouse for him tonight, eh Canada?" I recognized it immediately.

"Crawford!" I shouted as I spun around and jumped out of my seat, relieved that I wasn't the victim of some elaborate hoax. I shook his hand and pulled him close for a quick embrace and slap on the back. "Hey, great to see you man. I was beginning to wonder if anyone was going to show."

Crawford took the seat beside me. He still retained a boyish look about him although his body and particularly his face showed the effects of the large quantity of alcohol that had funnelled through him for decades. His cheeks were pudgy. His black hair was thinner and dishevelled. His eyes, puffy and red.

"Sorry I'm late, mate. I had some, um, luggage issues," he said glancing at the oversized black briefcase he placed gingerly on the floor next to him.

"Sure," I said, still annoyed at the delay, but not enough to cause a fuss. "No problem. So, where's the rest of the crew?"

"The crew, yes . . . well that's the thing of it. Merton isn't coming."

My eyes narrowed.

"You know that Lily had their second child last month, right?"

"Yes . . ." I said slowly, readying for the excuse. "I sent flowers."

"Well she has forbidden him from leaving the country. You know the standard, 'How am I supposed to cope with a newborn and a toddler all alone?' crap. Christ it's not like they don't have an *amah*," he said spitting out the last phrase. "And Armitage is still afraid of flying after the whole 9/11 thing. Won't get on a plane. Can you believe that? So he's staying put in Manchester."

"You're kidding me, right?"

"No - I'm not."

"Well, that's just fucking great," I said slowly enunciating the obscenity for full effect. Behind him I could see the mobile phone faceplate vendor grinning and laughing as if she had sensed what was going on and found the situation humorous. I gritted my teeth to contain the tirade of obscenities that I wanted to unleash. Surely Crawford had known all of this before tonight I thought. So why not just cancel the whole damn thing? I started to mentally add up how much this wasted trip was going to cost me in both lost vacation time and money.

"And," I said, making no attempt to hide my annoyance, "what's Rogers' bullshit excuse? After all this was his brilliant idea." I raised my empty glass into the air in mock imitation of our vow. "Five years hence!" I said in a bitterly sarcastic voice, not caring about the spectacle that I was making of myself.

Crawford's eyes avoided mine. His lips puckered unsurely. I waited for the excuse. He looked back at me and then, with the same matter-of-fact tone that he would use to tell me the colour of a new suit, calmly said, "Rogers' bullshit excuse?" He paused. "Rogers' bullshit excuse is that he's dead."

My eyes blinked hard as my brain refused to process what he had just said. I had expected a wide range of feeble excuses, anything from "he had a business trip to Malaysia," to "he couldn't afford to take time off." Death, however, had not made the list. Surely Crawford would have called or e-mailed us immediately if something had happened to Rogers. It had to be some kind of sick, pathetic joke. "What do you mean he's dead?" I said, not at all in the mood for a hoax.

"I mean he's *dead*. As in dead and buried. Actually no, check that. He's not buried - just dead." The calm in Crawford's voice was inconsistent with the news he was bestowing upon me and it was beginning to annoy me. I had always been a firm believer in the concept that one's demeanour should mirror the news that one bore.

"Look man, I've had a shitty flight, I'm jet-lagged and I'm . . ."

Crawford ignored my rant. He reached down into his briefcase, ruffled some papers, pulled out a small ceramic Chinese vase and placed it carefully in the centre of the table.

"There, that's better. Now, that's three of us here."

I didn't understand at first, but then Crawford's previous words echoed in my head. *He's not buried – just dead.* "Please tell me that, *that*," I said pointing to the vase, "is not what I think it is."

"I'm not sure what *you* think it is mate, but I can tell you what *it* is - it's Rogers."

Crawford spent the next hour answering the multitude of questions that cascaded from my now, much more sober mouth. What? When? How? The answers that came back – unlike the novels that drew us to Hong Kong - were devoid of any adventure or romance. There was no sky diving accident, high-speed chase or shoot out over a beautiful girl. There was no blaze of glory, just a slow wasting away. Not at all how Rogers wanted to go.

His testicular cancer had been diagnosed just before we left Hong Kong in '97 and did not respond to treatment. According to Crawford, that was why the reunion meant so much to him. It gave him something to live for. It also accounted for his sudden sentimentality. *I'm going to miss you guys.* The words echoed again through my head. His fight against cancer was buoyed most by the thought of one final "hurrah" in Hong Kong with the boys. It worked well. Even the doctors were amazed that he lasted so long. But it wasn't enough – he had died the week before I arrived. While on his deathbed Rogers swore Crawford to secrecy until we were all in Hong Kong.

"Come on," Crawford said rising from the table and gingerly placing the vase back into his briefcase. He nodded to the waitress who disappeared behind the bar before reappearing and handing Crawford a tall, unopened bottle of Scotch whiskey. "Thanks love, and, put my friend's beers on my tab." She nodded.

"Where are we going?" I asked.

"We've got to grab a taxi."

We picked our way through the crowded district. Groups of twenty-something males, ties askew, expensive looking suits drenched in sweat shouted "Hey" to friends passing by before clinking beer bottles and hoisting them to their lips. Their female counterparts slavishly adhered to the upscale Lan Kwai Fong dress code that called for heels (no panty hose) and short dresses of every colour under the rainbow, as long as it was black. At any other time, I would have revelled in the decadence of this scene; as the five of us had done for nearly twenty years. But, with Rogers' death, it was so sadly trite – an unreal world that I merely floated through as I followed Crawford to a stand of red taxis.

Crawford and I said very little to each other as our taxi began its ascent along a narrow, winding road cut from the rugged volcanic rock that formed Victoria Peak. For most of the short trip I stared out the window, my thoughts lost in the past.

Near the top, the driver bypassed the massive, concrete tourist lookout and followed another dimly-lit road to an old, broken mansion. Crawford told the driver to keep the meter running. The courtyard of the mansion projected over the edge of the mountain giving an unobstructed view of Hong Kong and Lan Kwai Fong below.

"Rogers found this place a few months ago," Crawford said. "Just before he got too bad. It's slated for demolition, but since the economy's gone pear-shaped, the developer is holding off." He paused. "Rogers thought it was a good place." Even after death Rogers was determined to go out with a flourish; he would get his jump from The Peak after all.

Crawford pulled the bottle of Scotch from his bag together with two shot glasses. He handed one to me after filling it. "Five years hence," Crawford said as he clinked his glass with mine. "Five years hence" I echoed. We downed our shots and pitched our glasses out into the night. There was an unusually strong wind pushing out into the harbour; trees swayed across the city lights; Star Ferries scooted across the glassy harbour; faint strains of music and laughter drifted up from below. I turned back when I heard Crawford rummage through his briefcase. I knew what was next.

"Give me a hand mate. I don't want to do this alone."

I grabbed the bottom of the vase with one hand, and together we took the few steps to the edge. We waited for the wind to pick up again, and then gently tilted it out over the abyss.

Will the Cycle Be Unbroken
by Shane Joseph

That dinner was like all the others we'd had at Christmas in the old country, or so I thought. Dad and Uncle Bunty at the table, talking politics, amidst opened bottles of arrack and soda; Mum frying more "taste" in the kitchen, while the main meal simmered on the kerosene stove. She was perspiring, and tired, but her men had to be provisioned. Ever since I remembered, Mum looked tired, and I felt sorry and helpless towards her. Dad was in his "jolly" mood that night, the alcohol expanding his spirits; the next day, he would sulk for hours when the effects wore off.

I was under the table, my usual safe place, driving imaginary race cars and swooping up occasionally to catch a devilled sprat from the fried taste bowl between the men. Their conversation had turned towards that dream place all Sri Lankan Burghers wanted to eventually "burgher-off" to – Australia, the land of milk and honey. That is, if you brought your own cows and bees, Dad's brother David, who had migrated ten years ago, wrote home and complained.

Australia, where one could afford to buy a house, car and other luxuries like TVs, stereos, washing machines, dryers, and stuff that would make life easier for Mum, Dad said in his jollier moments.

"Someone still has to cook. You bet I'll still be cooking over there." Mum could be heard through the wafting smells of beef curry and crackling fish.

"Yah, we'll all go together," Uncle Bunty said. "I'll go first. Then I'll sponsor all of you."

"You've been saying that for ten years," Mum said. "When are you going to get off your arse and do it?"

"All in good time. All in good time." Uncle Bunty said. I saw his legs twitch under the table. He usually got that way when the neighbours' servant boy raided our mango tree; the one

Uncle Bunty had planted and still tended with loving care. He came to live with us after his wife died giving birth to their only child, strangled in its umbilical cord. Left him scared of marrying again, Mum explained to me.

The first bottle of arrack was nearly empty and Uncle Bunty rhapsodized over the TV he would buy so that he could watch the test cricket. "Imagine, they have wide-screen colour sets over there and we don't even have bloody TV in this country. The international test cricketers won't even stop here on their way to India or Pakistan."

Dad drained the arrack bottle into the glasses and shouted to Mum, the edge returning to his voice. "Bring the other bottle. And what about the sprats? This bowl is almost empty."

"Christo boy is eating them under the table." Uncle Bunty said, appeasing, and swooping down playfully to grab me. I smelt his alcohol laden breath. Luckily, he was tipsy by now so I could dodge him easily. I liked him when he was sober; he read stories and played with me in the garden. When he was drunk, he only felt sorry for himself.

"Christopher, come and help child," Mum called again, her voice breaking slightly.

I parked my imaginary car, got out from under the table and went to her aid. She looked washed out - seven months pregnant and all. This was Christmas Eve, and at midnight, the neighborhood would explode with firecrackers. Dad and Uncle Bunty, too far gone by then, usually snored through the fireworks; however, I knew that each had bought me a toy, to be revealed when I opened the gifts tomorrow. But this was Mum's Christmas too, and all she did was work. I started to empty the potato and onion skins into the garbage.

"You know, you men should all bugger off to Australia. Then I can be at peace," Mum said. "Bunty, you may be my elder brother, but you have no balls, either."

"What the hell are you talking about?" Dad was slurping about her in the kitchen. "You will live like a queen, honey. None of this shit. This country is fucked up – at least for minorities like us."

81

Now, these many years later, I have figured out his motivations. He wanted to give Mum a good life despite his mood swings. But coming from a fast disappearing minority, and working as a clerk in a mercantile firm in the city, he could never rise in rank despite his best efforts. His ambitions had never been realized; and with the national language switching over from English to Sinhala, which he had never studied, his aspirations finally flamed out. He only thought of getting out, like many Burghers were doing at the time, but he wasn't successful at that either.

Australia was very attractive due to that country's accommodation of Asians of mixed European ancestry. Burghers, with their Dutch and Portuguese roots, fitted the bill perfectly. But all of Dad's applications had been turned down because of his erratic performances at immigration interviews, Mum said.

"Bloody Jansz up the road got passed. The bugger has not even got a grade six education. His welding is more recognized then my clerking!" And so Dad would rail against his misfortunes. And he irritated Mum a lot. I think he was irritated with himself too, that's why he was often depressed and drank to "drown his sorrows," Mum said.

Mum slapped his hands off the pan. "Wait till it's served. I put a lot of effort into this dinner – not for you to go fingering it."

"I'm hungry, no?" And he had that look in his eyes when he came home after drinks with the office crowd and I heard the bed bonk and Mum cry afterwards.

"All you men do is drink, eat, fuck and dream. You can't *do.*"

"Don't talk to me like that you ungrateful woman. I have tried. And there is nothing else to do but eat, drink and fuck in this shit hole."

"You can try by not being so smart at those interviews."

"Those white embassy bastards – they are prejudiced."

"And you want to go and live there?"

82

"Don't double talk me woman. I put bread on the table."

"And I bake it!"

"Sammy –" Uncle Bunty's voice came nervously from the hall. "What size TV will you buy when we get to Australia?"

"You are an ungrateful bitch," Dad said, taking a handful of beef from the pan and shoving it into his mouth...

The scene recedes. I am in a bed; a TV monitor hangs from the ceiling and the walls are light green. There are other beds on either side, with people in them and screens drawn around. I feel imprisoned. The Maple Leafs are playing the Flyers on television but I am not interested. A thickset middle-aged man in a trench coat walks into the room. His face is kindly, but he looks like he has seen a lot of trouble in the past.

"Inspector Martin." He offers me his card and pronounces his name, French-style. "Can I ask you a few questions?"

I nod. The bandages around my head and neck barely allow me to move and it hurts like crazy. The inspector pulls out a notebook and pen.

"Your name is Chris Martenstyn?"

Maybe talking is better than nodding. "Yes," I say and my voice is croaky.

"That's a Dutch name. It says that you were born in Sri Lanka."

He's just like the others – Canadians have no clue of our mixed up culture – they see a pile of Tamil immigrants in Toronto and think all Sri Lankans are dark skinned Dravidians.

"Yes. And I'm not Dutch – my ancestors were. A vanishing minority in Sri Lanka. "

"Employed?"

"Unemployed. Last two years."

"It says on the report that there was a domestic dispute. Your spouse –"

"Common-law -"

"Your companion, then. Ms. Bonnie Bagley. She assaulted you with a baseball bat?"

"Yes."

"Want to tell me about it?"

"No."

"This is a criminal investigation, Mr. Martenstyn."

"She called me a failure."

"Why?"

"I'm not a failure. Never was."

"Was it your unemployed status? No money coming into the family coffers? I've seen it before, Mr. Martenstyn."

"So we were backed up on the rent. And they reclaimed the car. So what?"

"Things must have been tight, financially."

"Well, unemployment insurance ran out. But I had a few odd jobs while Bonnie waited tables. It wasn't that bad."

"It says here, that you were both under the influence."

"It was Christmas Eve. It's not illegal to take a drink, is it?"

"No. So you had both been celebrating?"

My head feels like it is about to explode, but I have to keep going. "She was drinking to pluck the courage to say she was leaving me."

"Oh."

"She had it good when I was in the government job. Then they downsized. No one hires a government employee, you know."

"I should know. That's why I'll retire a cop."

"She called me a failure. I'm no failure. I came to this country on my own steam. Built my life here these past fifteen years. Even got a good job. I'm no failure."

"Do you have any family? Children?"

"No. Didn't want kids in this screwed-up world. She wanted kids. That was another reason she gave for leaving."

"Any siblings? Someone who can help you at this time?"

"No. I am an only child. My parents are dead, back in Sri Lanka. There was a still-born younger brother, and my old uncle Bunty, who is an alcoholic back home. No, I've got no one."

"How did you come to Canada?"

"After my mother died, I worked as a seaman on board a freighter. That was the only way out of Sri Lanka for a kid with a grade ten education. I left the ship in Halifax. Your system is so generous, they gave me asylum. I really wanted to go to Australia. But what does it matter – Australia, Canada, America, England – its freedom we wanted. Any port in the storm. I wish my mother was alive to know that I took the plunge, unlike my father and uncle. That's why I am not a failure."

"Do you want to tell me the rest of the story? Or do you want a defense attorney present."

"No. I'm glad it's over. I'll take whatever is to come."

"Why did Bonnie hit you?"

"Because she wanted me to react when she said she was leaving. Expecting me to try and hold on to her – but I didn't. Then she called me a failure. That's when I lost it. I slapped her. And she went at me with the bat."

"Has she been violent before?"

"I was attracted to her *because* she was violent. We first met in a pub ten years ago when she was brawling with another woman who'd been sleeping with her boyfriend at the time. Her boyfriend left her that night, despite Bonnie's brave performance. She was devastated. She reminded me of my father, who always wanted to go some place but no one would allow him, or believe in him. I took her back to my apartment and cleaned her wounds. We stuck together after that."

"You've had other violent incidents on record with Bonnie?"

"Several. But we kept it to ourselves. She's a manic depressive, like Dad. I took her beatings and rantings and stood it. I'd promised Mum, I wouldn't lift a finger to a woman. Bonnie was my test."

"What did you do after she hit you with the baseball bat?"

"Violence makes you lose your grip in the end – that much, I know now. This time, I broke my promise to Mum. And that's what I'm sorry about. But we all have our limits."

"What's your mother's connection to all this?"

"Leave her out of it!"

"Okay. Then what did you do?"

"I was bleeding. From my head, where she hit me. And it was all woozy. I remember the kitchen knife in my hand. My father flashed before me. Then I woke up in hospital."

"Bonnie's throat was slit and you had her blood all over the knife and you."

"I see. I killed her then."

"You may get a sympathetic jury. Self-defense would get you out. Manslaughter could get you a lighter sentence. You'll still make a second go of your life. If you survive prison."

"I've been in prison for a long time, Inspector. I'm just starting to be free."

He looks at me quizzically. Still making those notes in his book.

"Well, that's all we'll cover today. Get well soon. We'll need a formal statement tomorrow."

"Whenever…"

As he leaves the room that scene plays back again. It's been playing back too often lately. Perhaps the blow from the baseball bat has shaken loose my memory...

"You bastard, I told you not to eat that food." Mum took the pan of beef curry and threw the hot contents at Dad. It missed him and splashed all over the kitchen wall. "Eat bloody scraps tonight. I'm taking Christopher and going to my mother's place. You can celebrate Christmas with your bottles of arrack."

"You fucking bitch!" Dad howled, slapping her across the face.

"Sammy, Sammy..." Uncle Bunty came in pleading.

"You stay out of it, you son-of a bitch," Dad said.

Dad continued to pummel Mum on the head and I felt sick to my stomach. This was the worst I had seen him beat her. I ran across, caught Dad to pull him away from her. "Don't...leave her alone." He swung his wrist and the action sent me flying, knocking over the newly opened bottle of arrack and spilling its strong contents over the floor. Dad turned back to maul Mum again, when he stopped in his tracks like he was skewered. Mum was holding the knife that had plunged into his throat and emerged from the other side, the blood spurting all over, like water from the garden hose. The last thing I remembered before blacking out was Dad falling like a pole axed animal amidst the blood, arrack and beef curry; Uncle Bunty crawling all over him saying, " Sammy, don't die. I'm really sorry"; and Mum standing there remorselessly, holding her big belly and saying, "You don't have balls!"

I wish she were alive today, so I could write her one more letter, like the many I wrote while she languished in prison until her death.

"Mum, I understand how you felt that day. I *had* balls, and got out of the shit-hole. I wanted to break the cycle. But I guess I am my father's boy too. I carry both of you in me."

Moonlight on the Ligurian Sea: Travels With My Father
by Bill MacDonald

At the end of May, Felix and I flew to Milan, deplaned, and took the electric train south to Genoa. In our six-seat compartment, the only other passengers were two elderly Italian women, possibly sisters, who acknowledged us with disdainful glances and talked incessantly. When Felix said to them, "Buon giorno, signoras," they returned his greeting unsmilingly, pretended not to notice that their suitcases occupied both vacant seats as well as half the floor.

Early in the afternoon we disembarked at Genoa's Piazza de Principe train station. The first thing Felix did was try out his Italian on a taxi driver, who laughed and asked him in English where he wished to go.

"The Hotel Quezzi, per favore. On Via Venti Settembre."

"Si, signore," the driver scoffed, letting us carry our own bags. "I know where isa the Hotela Quezzi."

Unfortunately, we lasted only two nights at the smelly, threadbare, slightly mouldy Hotel Quezzi. From our room on the fifth floor we had a partial view of the fountain at Piazza de Ferrari, and if you went out on the balcony and craned your neck you could glimpse the gabled roof of the Carlo Felice Opera House. But most noticeable was the ear-splitting racket from the street below - thundering buses, screaming motorcycles, car horns, sirens, musicians under the arches blaring away on amplified saxophones. With our window open, the din was overwhelming. With it closed, Felix feared suffocation. When I awoke with a start at two a.m., thinking we were under attack, I found him sitting on the edge of his bed, fingers in his ears, looking frightened. "What the hell have I got us into, Sport? We can't stay here. We won't get a moment's rest. Don't these people ever sleep?"

Next morning, jet-lagged, on edge, braving misty drizzle and exhaust fumes, we toured the city in a double-decker bus. We saw the Ducal Palace and the ancient church of San Teodoro, both of which disappointed Felix. He was especially chagrined at not seeing the palatial 19th century homes on Via Garibaldi, but since the war, Via Garibaldi has been closed to vehicular traffic. When I suggested that we might do better on foot, Felix complained of headache, lethargy, chest pains, said it was out of the question. Finally, at Piazza Acquaverde, under the statue of Christopher Columbus, we dismounted. At a dockside café, under tattered umbrellas, we took shelter from the rain, ordered glasses of industrial-strength grappa. Though the harbour bustled with all manner of boats, which should have pleased him, and damp cyclists in red jerseys raced by, Felix said he regretted having come all the way to Italy for nothing. "It isn't what I expected, Sport. Noise, crowds, bad plumbing."

So next day we took a cab to Stazione Brignole and caught the commuter coach to Santa Margherita, twenty kilometres further up the Ligurian coast. Just as we arrived, the sun came out, the Mediterranean sparkled.

We spent two weeks in sleepy Santa Margherita, at the Hotel Desiderio, on a rocky cliff above the sea. Pine and palm trees rose as high as our third-floor balcony. Potted viburnum plants covered every windowsill, hung from every trellis, shedding red berries and aromatic white petals. Though probably older than the Hotel Quezzi in Genoa, and showing signs of decay, the Desiderio was quiet, breezy, full of wicker chairs and ceiling fans. The wrought iron railings on its patio needed paint, its slate floors were cracked and uneven. But still, it was a comfortable, matronly hotel, unashamed of its shabbiness, making no pretense to be modern. There were bleached shutters on its seaward windows, dysfunctional fountains in its overgrown courtyard. The desk clerk, Antonio, a white-haired gentleman in yellow shoes and royal blue jacket, seemed genuinely pleased to see us. His English, though heavily accented, was comprehensible. He assigned us a window table in the dining room, pointed out that it had the best view of the sea and shoreline. When he saw we were pleased, he escorted us into the creaking elevator and took us up to our room, whose gilt-trimmed door he unlocked with a tarnished key. He opened the casement windows, threw back the shutters, stood there inhaling deep drafts of air, as though he were the guest and Felix the hotelier.

"You lika thisa room, signores? Thisa hotel?"

"We like it," Felix said. "You don't have to sell us. We'll stay. After Genoa, this is paradise. Paradiso."

"Ah, Genoa, signore. Isa bigga city. Too mucha crazy people. In Santa Margherita, isa nicea place for relax."

Felix was content to walk the town's streets and piazzas, looking at churches and fountains, sitting in sidewalk cafés. He used his meagre Italian on old men basking in the sun, who, though puzzled by him, were tolerant. Most mornings, he enjoyed having his breakfast on the hotel terrace, looking down at the sea, tossing bread to the gulls. If he found beetles on the starched white tablecloth or in the sugar bowl, he flicked them into the bougainvillea bushes. He grew to like espresso in a demitasse and complained only mildly about cold toast and watery eggs. He became good friends with Antonio, and with Benedetto, the hotel bartender, and with Doria, our mustachioed chambermaid. He worried that I'd be bored, but I wasn't. I slept late, read newspapers at breakfast, swam in the saltwater pool below the cliff. Some days I accompanied him on his strolls about town, treated him to a glass of Cinzano on Via Marconi. We bought the Herald Tribune and two or three British tabloids at a kiosk on Piazza Trieste. Most afternoons I read or napped on our balcony, lulled by birdsong, the lapping of waves, the perfume of flowers.

One afternoon when I came up from swimming, I found Felix on the terrace, sipping iced Amoroso, engaged in conversation with a refined-looking woman his own age. She was wearing a white summer dress and a straw sun hat, and had a cane at her side. When he saw me, Felix called me over, introduced me to his new friend, Signora Caterina Luccoli, a retired school teacher from Torino. Signora Luccoli, it turned out, had been coming to the Hotel Desiderio for many years, on the anniversary of her honeymoon. Unfortunately, her husband Ettore, who no longer recognized her, was presently in a nursing home in Torino, suffering from senility. The fact that he had no idea who she was, or that he was married to her, made it seem senseless to forgo her annual holiday in Santa Margherita. Did Felix not agree? Of course he did. How could she, an elegant, fascinating woman, celebrate her anniversary with someone unaware of her identity?

Felix's and Signora Luccoli's backgrounds were amazingly similar. Both had taught high school English. During their careers, both had published slim volumes of poetry. Both had married during the war. Both had personal childhood secrets they didn't share with just anyone. Both had been deserted (though in different ways and through no fault of their own) by their respective spouses.

It wasn't long before Felix and Caterina were having breakfast together, then lunch, then cocktails and afternoon tea. He gave up walking about town, spent the entire day with her, sitting on the terrace, hovered over by Antonio and Benedetto. He would offer her his arm and the two of them would meander about the grounds like an old married couple. At dinner, Caterina sometimes sat at our table, we sometimes sat at hers. After dessert, she and Felix would take chairs under the palm trees on the terrace, smoke cigarettes, watch fishing boats put out to sea.

Signora Caterina Luccoli left Santa Margherita by train a day before we did. At our last dinner, after a litre of wine, she and Felix got into an argument over whether Ophelia should be praised or pitied. That led to a heated discussion of unfaithful literary heroines, such as Flaubert's Emma Bovary and Tolstoy's Anna Karenina - an area in which both Caterina and Felix claimed personal experience. At the mention of Flaubert, Caterina asked whether it wasn't he who had said of old age, "Life! Life! Oh, to have erections!" Then she asked Felix why he'd never written anything but poetry. Why not a novel?

"Because," he said, "writers of novels are nothing but parrots, mimicking what they hear. Actually, novelists are worse than parrots, because parrots you can at least throttle. Besides, I lacked a muse. To write novels, you need a muse. The only muse I had was an unfaithful wife, and all she inspired were poems of loss and regret. My one and only marriage left me incapable of many things, including trusting women and writing novels. Still, many men don't trust women or write novels, yet do quite well in life."

Caterina smiled, reached for her cane. "Forgive me, signores," she said, rising stiffly. "Thisa timea tomorrow I am ina Torino, sitting at the bedside of my poor Ettore, telling him there are no tigers ina his closet."

Next morning Felix went with her by taxi to the train station. When he came back he was morose, depressed. He'd suggested she stay one more day, take a picnic lunch to

Portovenere, but she'd said no. He'd offered to accompany her to Torino. Again she'd said no. She refused to give him her address, or accept his. "I don'ta writa letters," she'd said. "I used to, but now, no. My eyes are nota so good."

It rained hard that night. Dark clouds rolled down off the surrounding hills at sunset, bringing thunder and lightning. Gusts of wind swept across the bay and surf began pounding the cliff below the hotel. The shutters on our west window banged against the wall and Felix got soaked fastening them. On our balcony and down on the patio you could hear deck chairs being blown about.

Next morning the sun shone and the bay was full of sailboats. They seemed to be preparing for some sort of regatta. After breakfast, having decided to bypass Genoa on our return trip, we took a taxi to the train station and bought first class tickets for the noon Express to Milan. We found benches on the platform, sat watching a group of school children board coaches headed in the opposite direction. It was Felix's theory that they were on a field trip to see the leaning tower of Pisa.

It was during our train ride through the verdant countryside of northern Italy that Felix admitted a growing fear of loneliness. He was afraid, he said, not so much of living alone, as of dying alone. He guessed it was a fear most old people had. He said that when he thought about it, he sometimes came close to panic. In the middle of the night, he'd wake up, terrified. He said he'd been thinking of Signora Luccoli's husband, but felt no pity for him, because he'd taken the easy way out, trading loneliness for insanity.

We rode on in silence, thinking our own thoughts, looking out at the green hills speeding by, at the quarries and factories and houses with red tiled roofs. Finally, as we rounded a curve, we saw the turquoise locomotive pulling us, and beyond it, against the sun, the hazy, uninviting suburbs of Milan. High above floated the vapour trails of westbound jets.

I saw little of Felix during the summer. After our return from Italy, we were both busy. In September, at his insistence, we started having lunch together every Thursday at the Café Delfino on Bay Street. He would come downtown by bus from Gull's Wing Retirement Home, do his banking, sip a Coors Lite at our corner table in the Delfino.

But one cold Thursday in late November, he didn't show up. It wasn't like him to forget lunch dates. I waited for him till one-thirty, thinking he might have missed his bus, and finally telephoned nurse McQuilter at Gull's Wing. Yes, Felix MacDonald was still in his room. No, she didn't know why he hadn't gone downtown. Would I like to speak to him?   "No," I said. "If you don't mind, I'll drive out."

I found him sitting in his chair by the window, staring at the leafless elm trees. At first, I thought he was asleep. But he wasn't. Without turning his head, he knew by some strange telepathy that I was there.

"I couldn't make it, Sport. I tried, but I couldn't do it. I was going to phone and tell you, but I lay down for a minute, and when I woke up, I knew you'd be on your way. I'm sorry."

His voice was feeble, quavering. I'd never heard it like that before. He said he'd been having dizzy spells all week, as recently as that morning. He said he'd stayed in bed and missed breakfast. I asked him if he'd informed nurse McQuilter, or seen a doctor, and he said no, he hadn't. What was the use? They'd already told him he was on the verge of renal failure and would soon have to go downtown for dialysis three times a week. They'd need to put a valve in his arm. He said, "They think it's my kidneys, Sport, which are only functioning at half speed. First, they told me I had pneumonia. Then Spanish flu. What a bunch of knuckleheads. All my strength is gone, Sport. Drained out of my feet. Left me like a dishrag. And I've had this feeling of impending doom. Ever had that? I'm pretty sure I've got a terminal brain tumour. A big one. It would explain my symptoms. I can feel it in there, growing bigger every day, crowding out my grey matter."

The most difficult days were the ones on which he didn't recognize me. He would stare out the window, shake his head, mutter to himself. Sometimes he told me that an old woman with a cane was in the habit of coming in and reading to him. One day, after visiting him, I asked nurse McQuilter when his dialysis would start. She said she knew nothing about it.

"He told me his kidneys had quit working."

"Well, I assure you, they haven't. That's not to say they won't. What else has he told you?"

"That he has a brain tumour. That he has no circulation in his legs. That someone stole his driver's license. That there's a surveillance camera in his room."

"You'll have to start taking everything your father says with a grain of salt. None of that is true. I'm not saying he doesn't have a brain tumour. Or faulty kidneys. He may very well have. They just haven't been diagnosed. He may also be a rocket scientist. He might win the lottery. But then again, he might not. Who knows?"

The night before he died, Felix held my hand, which was something he'd never done. The only person I'd ever seen him hold hands with was my mother, and that was a long time ago. I could hear his breathing becoming very shallow, as though he didn't need much air. When I looked out his window, I saw that it was snowing. While we were in Italy, one thing he'd said he missed was snow. We were having drinks one evening on the terrace of the Hotel Desiderio in Santa Margherita, arguing over whether the surrounding, sweet-smelling flowers were viburnum or bougainvillea, and Felix had said that if you used your imagination, the silver carpet of moonlight shimmering across the bay looked like snow. It struck me as an odd time to be thinking of snow.

"Isn't this beautiful enough for you?" I said. "If you wanted snow, you should have gone to the Alps."

"I only meant I'm a bit homesick, Sport. No need to get huffy. Of course, it's beautiful."

At the time, it seemed a senseless argument to be having. Perhaps we'd drunk too much wine at supper. But now, in his room at Gull's Wing, watching real snow, I felt I knew what he'd meant. To us, snow was familiar, reassuring. You could, if you wanted to, go walking in it. Mediterranean moonlight, while lovely to look at, was deceptive.

Early next morning, nurse McQuilter phoned me. I knew before she spoke that Felix had died. She said he'd gone peacefully, in his sleep. "Count your blessings, young man," she said, but I have no idea what that meant.

Gone Tomorrow
by Deborah Cannon

Only three of us survive. We are waiting for the ships. I don't know what our fate will be, don't dare predict. It happened so fast.

The sliding door of the airlock opened, sending my heart into warp drive. Oh Lord. The hound from hell. Lu Mare, our captain and the station's ecologist, tossed her helmet to the deck and opened her arms. From one of the passageways in the Martian station, a big yellow puppy galloped up. It stood on its hind quarters trying to grab her face with its paws. She ruffled the dog's fur and planted a big kiss on the top of his head while I cringed.

"What's the matter, Jordan? Nostradamus is just a pup. He can't hurt you."

I showed Nostradamus a trembling hand, and instead of sniffing it, he dived into my face.

"You okay?"

I shuddered, lied. "I'm fine. Is David here?"

"He's out collecting samples, but he'll be back for chow."

I had just arrived from the Agaricus II one of the biospheres orbiting Mars. Lu Mare had picked me up at the landing and brought me to the Ranunculus. It was not a large station, but it was home for the next six months. It was constructed like a torpedo or a submarine, and like a submarine, it had only one entrance.

Lu pointed to a door. "You're bunking with me, so the cube's empty. I've got to complete some reports, but if you want some company—" Her eyes flew briefly to Nostradamus before returning to mine. I shook my head quickly and entered the cube.

Outside the only porthole, Olympus Mons rose above the Tharsis plains. In the nearby sea, squat columnar stromatolites, pink, green and blue jutted out of the backwash. Waves sloshed and sucked, heaved up and out, and splashed the coral and sulphur sand mottling the shore. Dust swirled, burst, as a hovercraft scuttled by. Two faint moons showed above the settling dust, and somewhere beyond that . . . was Earth.

David and I were lovers on Earth. I will never forget the dark look on his face the last time I saw him. The growl, the terrified voice. David jerking his head up from the tray of green slime that was meant for the simulator. My own voice screaming. I remember seeing him through the window of the lab as he shoved the glass tray into the simulator. He had left the hatch open and come outside, approached the snarling boxer, held its collar, then let go, and put an arm around me and walked me indoors. A snarl had come from behind us. His boxer skulked in. David went for its collar, too late. The dog lunged at me. As I dodged its snapping jaws, it catapulted into the simulator and I slammed the hatch shut. In my panic to get away, I tripped onto the console, switching it on. The dog convulsed, its eyes bulged, and its blood boiled. Then the body of David Wang's boxer crumpled in the simulated Martian air.

Nauseated at the memory, I forced my attention back to the porthole. Accidents happened. That sea and that sky. Stromatolites on Mars. That was why I was here, and why Mars, given enough time, would look like Earth.

A scratching started at the door, then a whining and a whimper. Nostradamus was sniffing at the threshold. I could hear him, almost smell him. If humans had hackles, mine were rising. The hairs along my arms bristled. Gooseflesh rippled across my shoulders. A man's voice mumbled, then a scurrying of canine claws followed. I waited, opened the door, and peered into the corridor. There was no dog and no David either. I braced a hand on the bulkhead and shut the heavy door behind me. When I turned around, I almost screamed.

Lu had materialized from nowhere.

"What's the matter, you got the jitters? You're probably suffering from shuttle sickness. It'll pass with a good night's sleep." She squinted down one of the narrow passageways and motioned for me to follow. "Let's go visit the cairn. David won't be back for another hour. You look like you need something to do; you're so pale."

Nostradamus was curled up, asleep, on the deck in front of the airlock. We tugged on our suits and fastened our helmets, and just as we entered the airlock, the dog stirred. He glanced up, stretched, and Lu blocked his abrupt leap with her knee and sent the sliding door shut in his face.

The two faint moons hung on the horizon. Red dust whirled around my mask, and I turned from the wind to seek out the cairn which sat on the Martian beach, a mound of grey stones.

The wind was gusting harder and Lu brushed dust from her mask. I stared at the baleful sky, then looked back at Lu, who pointed to the entrance of the cairn. Dropping to my knees, I peered into the dark hole and tried to crawl in, but my shoulders jammed with the thick suit. I gestured with a hand. Had she been inside? I'd been told that there were bones in there, and unless I could remove my suit without dying a horrible, gruesome death, Lu, who was shorter and thinner, and altogether smaller, would have to retrieve them for me. But that would have to wait for a calmer day.

David was in the computer lab when we returned. He looked the same. His black hair was styled in a neat brush cut. His intelligent eyes made me feel like I knew less about everything than he did. He was lean and muscular, and his umber skin was blemish free. He looked up briefly, only long enough to recognize me, then he returned to his simulation on the computer.

From the counter, he lifted a vial of blue green algae. Life first emerged on Earth about 3.5 billion years ago. The same had occurred on Mars a billion years earlier. Then a meteor had stopped evolution in its tracks. All of that had been buried under rock and ice. Now, life was forming again; there was algae in the seas.

He replaced the vial, tapped at the console; the soft silicone keys made no sound. A giant simulated comet made its fiery way across the screen, the brilliant tail fragmenting into pieces as it struck the earth's orbit.

"The universe never ceases to amaze me."

My comment was met with silence. "Lu took me to see the hominid bones today. I couldn't get inside the cairn, but I used the remote camera and got some wonderful images. The bones are definitely those of a female. I think she was alone . . ."

I watched the side of his face for any sign that he was listening. "Can you imagine how frightened she must have been when it happened, if she saw the meteor coming? Of course the chances are she didn't see it and if she did she wouldn't have understood what it meant, so she wouldn't have been afraid—" I broke off, suddenly realizing that we hadn't seen each other in two years. "Hello David," I murmured.

David remained mute. He ran a new scenario and this time when the comet struck Earth, one quarter of the planet exploded.

I winced.

His face stayed fixed, stern, as he ran another scenario. This time he replaced Earth with a simulated Mars and filled the red planet with greenery—what Mars might have looked like when the hominids were alive. Then he changed the comet to a meteor. On impact, everything shrivelled up and died. He fast-forwarded the simulation, and life started forming again, blue-green algae . . .

"Here so fast, gone so fast." My voice was a strangled whisper.

David turned to me with an exasperated look on his face. Yes, I had been talking too much.

"Everything we had to say to each other was said two years ago. What are you doing here, Jordan, except running my ear off, babbling about things I already know."

"I was assigned to study the bones in the cairn."

"Then study them. But stay away from me, and stay away from my dog."

At dinner that evening, he avoided my eyes and spoke only to Lu. For the first time since we had met, the captain was quiet. She looked from me to David and screwed up her face. She opened her mouth like she wanted to ask what the hell was going on between us, but nothing came out.

David left the mess hall for the gym.

I went to the lockers to suit up.

A snuffling caught my attention and Nostradamus came around the corner, eyes gleaming with joy, tail wagging wickedly.

Go away! I yanked on my helmet, almost snapping my wrist, and stepped into the airlock. Nostradamus followed. No! I chased him around the airlock but he thought it was a game. A few seconds later David entered, sweat flying from his workout. He seized Nostradamus by the collar and sent him out. Then he hiked up my mask and glared at me.

That night I awoke to voices on the other side of the bulkhead.

"What the hell is going on between you and Jordan?"

"Nothing. Nothing that concerns you."

"Everything that happens on this station concerns me."

"We had a past, okay? Let's leave it at that."

"I will not leave it at that. Don't you realize how serious this is? I need you to have your mind on the job. Fix whatever's messed up between you, and help her study those bones in the cairn. I want the both of you to figure out what happened here and the probability of it happening again."

"Don't you understand? I can't work with her."

"Find a way. You may only have one chance, David, so seize it while you can."

"I've been calculating probabilities, Lu, running scenarios for two years. Nothing's changed."

"And Mars wasn't supposed to start growing life."

The next morning they were gone before I awoke. I went to the locker to suit up. A reflection flickered in the corner of my mask and I blinked. I couldn't see much because the helmet had too many blind spots. I passed through the airlock to the outside, and before I could even react, Nostradamus flew past me.

Wind lashed viciously at my suit, dust swirled.

Horrified, I scoured the landscape, but the dog was gone.

By my stance and total inability to answer the hail over the transmitter, David knew something was wrong. He saw me from the beach and ran clumsily toward me. When he reached the station he rushed past me to the airlock. I tried to stop him from entering, but we were already in and the door shut. A minute passed, the air equalized and the inner door slid open. David shot into the corridor. He searched his cube and under his bunk. He went to the mess, the lab, the gym. He grabbed me, and turned me to face him, his glare accusing, while tears rained down my cheeks.

"He's not here."

He brushed me aside, passed through the airlock and went outside with me at his heels. I snatched at his arm, but he tore away. The storm was rising, and I knew that there was only one place Nostradamus could find shelter—if he was still alive.

I made for the cairn, and David followed. The opening was black, but something bolted out of it, knocking me down. Overjoyed, David lunged for his dog but missed, and Nostradamus disappeared.

Then he poked his head out.

I couldn't hear a thing with my helmet on, but I could see the dog barking furiously. Delirious with relief, and with a sudden delayed flash of insight, I unfastened my helmet. I knew I was taking a huge chance, especially when David shouted, "NO!" But my helmet was already on the ground, my suit was off, and I was worming my way into the cairn.

Under the stone ceiling, Nostradamus huddled among the bones. I went to him, breathless, and soon, David appeared at the cairn's entrance, minus his gear, and crawled to us. I smiled idiotically, stroking Nostradamus's ears.

David watched us, overcome with relief, and ran an affectionate hand over his dog.

Abruptly, he raised his head, clipping his scalp on the stone ceiling, and caught my eyes. His own sparkled with excitement. "Yesterday the atmosphere would've killed us! I checked the instruments last night. Nitrogen, CO_2 levels were too high. My projection was for another decade before the air was thick enough to breathe. It must have been the new species of algae. When I tested that sample last night it gave off an explosive charge of pure oxygen, the most perplexing thing I've ever seen. This morning it was everywhere, a massive blue-green bloom covering the entire sea, an oxygen-emitting algal bloom."

A rattling started on the roof and I cupped my head. I curled up on the floor of the cairn and shut my eyes. The bones of the ancient hominid dug into my cheek. The pounding came heavier. Then, just as quickly as it had begun, the rattling stopped.

David and I exchanged puzzled glances and we crept outside to a strange sight. The ground was wet and hail the size of my fists lay melting all around.

He whistled in astonishment, toeing the ground. Miraculously, there were shoots breaking through, and what once was dust was now damp soil. He shooed Nostradamus ahead of us and grabbed my hand. "Come on, we'd better get back to the station and tell Lu."

I hesitated, bit my lip.

David squeezed my hand and kissed my forehead. It was amazing to feel his touch again, bare lips against bare skin.

I opened my eyes and saw the captain on the slope, suited up, agitated, beckoning for us to hurry. David let me go, and motioned for Lu to remove her helmet.

At once she realized what had happened to the atmosphere and raised her mask. As we got closer, she peered around, eyes wide, then her face changed.

A strange, eerily purple darkness was forming in the sky. Earth was just visible, a glowing blue orb. I looked at the captain and the pain on her face turned my chest cold. I was terrified to ask.

"How much time do they have?"

"Not enough. Your projections were off, David. The comet is coming sooner than we thought."

David gave an agonized cry, slumping to his knees.

Lu yanked him to his feet. "No time for mourning past mistakes. We'd better get ready for those who make it here."

The Race
by M. Bahgat

The first thought that came to Ahmed's head when he woke up that morning was the race. He stretched his brown body for a few seconds, and then got up. He was sure he would do well in swim meet. It did not start until five in the evening. In the morning, he was to go to the school as usual. Ahmed went to the Junior High school.

He finished his morning routine and went to the kitchen. He greeted his mother and his little brother, and joined them at the kitchen table. His mother put a plate of eggs and toast in front of him and said, "Are you ready for the big race?"

He looked at her and said, "I am ready."

He finished his meal, put his backpack on, and said goodbye.

When he left the townhouse and walked in the cool morning air, he was full of vigour and hope. He was keyed up about the coming race, and could hardly wait. He walked in long, easy strides with a smile on his face. When he was half way to the school, the smile vanished. His walking rhythm slowed down. The more he came closer, the more he felt a sense of doom. When the school came into sight, a feeling of gloom besieged him.

###

"What's going on down there?" shouted Mrs. Hoyle, the teacher.

Amy, a blond, twelve-year-old girl cried. "He kicked me, Mrs. Hoyle."

"Ahmed," said the teacher, "how could you do that? Kick a girl!"

His face was red, and tears swelled in his big, brown eyes. He said, in a Middle Eastern accent, "She kicked me first. I told her to stop, but she keeps on kicking me."

"Kept on," corrected Mrs. Hoyle.

Amy said, "He's lying. I didn't kick him, did I, John?"

John's green eyes twinkled as he said, "She didn't, Mrs. Hoyle."

He came beside Ahmed. With his right hand he removed a sheet of paper that was taped on Ahmed's back. He put his hand behind his back.

"What's that in your hand?" said the teacher, "Give it to me."

In a slow motion, John gave her the sheet of paper. He shook his shoulders and said, "We're just playing a joke."

Mrs. Hoyle looked at the sheet of paper. In large letters, it read, "Kick me."

Mrs. Hoyle blue eyes sparkled as she shouted, "How dare you do that in my class? Go back to your seats, all of you."

John and Amy turned around, and walked to their seats. They smiled slyly to the other children in the class.

Ahmed did not move. He said, "Is this all you gonna do? They put a sign on my back, they kicked me, and you don't punish them? It's no fair."

"How dare you question how, or whom I should punish?.Go back to your seat."

"It no fair."

"It isn't fair," righted the teacher, "Go back to your seat."

"It isn't fair," Ahmed shouted, and stamped his foot on the floor.

"Now you're going to leave this room, and go the principal's office."

Ahmed turned around, walked out of the classroom, and slammed the door behind him.

As soon as he was out of the classroom, tears that were held back by sheer pride came down. He sniffled as he walked. Now he was really going to get it. The principal will call home, and his father would be mad. He would say, "You must respect the teacher, no matter what." If Amy or John were called to the principal's office, they would not care. Their parents would likely give hell to the teacher, not to their children.

Ahmed took a paper tissue from his pocket and wiped the tears off his face. He sat for half an hour before he was allowed in the vice-principal's office. Ahmed was relieved that he did not have to see the principal.

Mr. Jones, tall, lean, and gray haired, looked kindly at the tall strong boy. "Well, Ahmed, you're having problems again."

"It wasn't my fault Mr. Jones. It's John and Amy. They have been on my case since I came to this school. They bugged me, made fun of my accent, and they call me names. Today, John put a sign on my back that says, 'Kick me', and they did. I told them to stop it, but they laughed at me. I pushed John away, but Amy kept kicking me. When she wouldn't stop, I kicked her back. I had to, don't you see?"

Mr. Jones gently said, "You were rude to the teacher."

"The teacher wouldn't do anything about it. It isn't fair."

"Ahmed, you must trust your teacher. I'm sure she was going to talk to John, later on."

Ahmed put his head down and did not say anything.

The vice-principal said, "Go back to your class. I'll talk to John and Amy."

Ahmed went back to bear the sneering looks and smiles of John, Amy and the others. Thank God, Mrs. Hoyle was not giving any more classes that day. There was another teacher in the room. Ahmed sat at his desk, but did not hear anything the teacher said. When the school was over, he walked home, alone.

When he arrived at home before his brother, his mother asked him the usual question, "How's school?"

Tears came down his face as he shouted, "I hate the school. I hate all the kids, all the teachers and the principle. Why did we leave Egypt?"

His mother hugged him and said, "Hush, hush, what's that all about? Is this boy hassling you again?"

He told her what happened. When he finished she said, "I'm proud of you, Ahmed. You stood up for you rights. You didn't let these boys scare you."

"They don't scare me. The other day John bothered me on the way home and I gave it to him. If it weren't for his two friends who were with him and who ganged up on me, I'd have broken his face. He never bothered me outside the school since. Only when he's in school and his friends are around that he dares bother me."

"That's my boy. Now go wash your face, get something to eat, and then get some rest before your father comes home."

When his father came, he did not have time for a proper meal. He only took a sandwich, and a cup of coffee and they left the house.

"Ahmed," said his father as they drove away, "we're all proud of you. I'm very proud of you. You've proved yourself to be a top swimmer, both back home, and in our new country. You

104

have reached provincial time in the two hundreds and the four hundreds meters free. Today you're going for the fifteen hundreds race. Your time in Egypt was already provincial time in Canada, and this was six months ago. You should get first place tonight."

Ahmed sat in silence, looking at the road ahead.

When they reached the pool, Ahmed went to the dressing room; his father went to the gallery to watch the race.

Ahmed put on his swimsuit, took a shower, and took his bag and went on deck. He was assaulted by the smell of chlorine, and the deafening sounds of the meet—loud cheers, whistles, and clapping. He stopped at the door and felt scared. It was a feeling he has never had before.

He walked on deck, going to where his team members were. All around him were white bodies, and fair hair. When Ahmed joined his team; he was the only boy with brown skin. Soon it was the warm up, and then the girls' races.

Ahmed sat, alone. The other children were talking, teasing each other, or playing cards.

The coach, Terry, called him. He put his arm around his shoulder and said, "Ahmed, I'm counting on you to get us a medal. You just go as fast as you did in practice last week. No one in the meet could come close."

Ahmed did not say anything and looked sadly around him. It was then that the loud speaker announced marshalling the boys. Without a word, he left the coach and went to the marshalling table.

A few minutes later, he was sitting on a chair waiting for his race. There were eight boys in his heat, the fastest. They were all white except him.

"What's your time?" asked the boy next to him.

Ahmed looked at the boy, then looked the other way.

The boy said, "I've never seen you in any race before."

"I did it in 20:05." Ahmed shot back, though he tried to keep quiet.

"Ha," snorted the boy, "Where did you do that?"

"In Egypt."

The boy snorted again, and said, "Egypt! No one heard of a time like that in Egypt, of all the places."

Before Ahmed could answer, they were signalled to go to the starting blocks.

They lined up; Ahmed put his goggles on, but his heart was heavy. The starting gun went off, and the boys dived into the water. They all came to the surface, swinging their arms, feet whipping, churning the water.

Ahmed kicked hard and fast. His arms hit the water in sturdy strokes. He was pulling ahead of the other boys. Feet by feet, he saw the bodies fall behind. When he came to the wall at the end of the first fifty meters, he was almost a body's length ahead. He made a perfect flip-turn, and gained a foot.

"I'll show them," he thought as he started to pace himself for the long race. Then the cruel, mocking faces of John and Amy flashed in his head. What difference does it make to them if I win or lose? he thought. He is the first of the class in math. It was not much help; they hated him more.

"It isn't fair." His eyes became moist from anger at being shunned out. What made it worse was that he did not know why.

Then he saw the wall, and he was not ready. He made a hasty turn, but it was not good. When he pushed off the wall, the other bodies caught up to him. From then on, he lost ground all the time. When he saw the white body of the boy who sat next to him pull ahead, his eyes were filled with tears. It clouded his vision, and made him slow down more.

He knew, his father would be mad at him. "How could you do that?" his father would shout, "How could you let your team down, your coach, and me?"

Ahmed shouted back, "My team! Why do I care about them? Did they ever care about me? I can't do it Daddy, I won't."

He did not know how the time went by. At the last hundred meters the bell rang. The chimes seemed to have awakened something in his head. He started to push himself. It was nothing new to him; he was not even tired, and he was used to pushing himself. This is not for them, he thought, it is for me and my Dad, and maybe the coach.

The leading boy was the one who sat next him at the marshalling area. He was now two bodies' length ahead of him. Ahmed kicked faster. His arms pushed back the water, as he has never done before. When they came to the wall, the leading boy was only one body's length to the fore.

Ahmed made a perfect flip-turn. He was now breathing hard. It is now do or die, he thought to himself. He was gaining on the leading boy with every arm stroke he made. When they were half way to the end, Ahmed was neck to neck with him. He pushed harder and the other boy pushed. Ahmed was out of breath, but he found some inner power in him. Now the wall loomed at them. Ahmed kicked harder, and his arms moved faster. When he hand hit the wall, he was ahead.

He raised his head from the water and took big gulps of the air. The rowdy sounds of cheers were sweet in his ears. He raised his hand in the air and waved to his father.

Perhaps

by Gabriella Papic

John Peel was dead. After a lengthy illness, John Peel, 56, died at Burlington's Mercy Hospital yesterday morning. I read the obituary three times, searching for hidden clues about the life of the man who made me a woman one vital December evening.

The first time I met John Peel, I was a college intern at the Burlington Herald. John, editor-in-chief at the time and my supervisor, kept me busy with his daily mission chart that carried the same three assignments every day: weapon maintenance, data interment, and elixir logistics for the troops. But as a nineteen year old with a dream, I was in a hurry to make my mark on the world, and with more than a noteworthy amount of arrogance, I created my own mission chart to quicken my ascension through the ranks. In just ten business days I had not unfairly earned the nickname Oh Susanna for my photo-copy-room escapades with a growing number of, what I deemed to be, influential men at the newspaper.

Intercourse-in-kind, at least in a verbal sense, finally transpired with John amidst a heap of winter coats in the guest bedroom of the publisher's mansion at the yearly Christmas party.

Earlier that evening, I had harvested my third drink from the waiter's silver platter when John called me a juvenile delinquent. I stood on the very tips of my black stiletto heels and in front of the publisher, his wife and all their guests, I raised my martini glass and slowly poured very expensive vodka over John's golden locks. Our breath met in a moment swollen with possibility. John clenched his hands over my bare upper arms to steady me and brushed his right palm close to my breast. He leaned in, whispering in my ear, his starched white collar close enough to touch my lips.

"Susan," he said. "You're drunk. Trust me, you don't want it to happen like this."

He released my arms and left me swaying in the middle of the room. The heat of embarrassment and desire burned in my chest and I headed for the bedroom to retrieve my coat and call a cab.

Coats of every possible size and colour lay heaped upon the grand brass and mahogany bed. With such force did I wrench out my satin and wool wrap that it caught on the polished ceiling fan above, and dangled from the rafters, much like my wounded pride. I turned to leave and found John standing in the doorway, his navy winter coat slung over one arm, and a yellow cashmere scarf already draped around his neck.

"Come on," he said, "I'm taking you home."

I went silently to him and kissed him, my lips parted, my tongue searching. I kissed him like I was eating a huge wet piece of watermelon. John clenched my arms once again and held me away from his body.

"Susan," he said, "you are better than this."

Once more he tightened his grip; I saw and felt him swallow hard. Then he released me, and walked out. I followed him to the car, got in, and sat shocked in silence as he drove me home. I quit my internship the next morning over the telephone.

Six years passed before I saw John again for the next and last time. Newly minted with a masters degree in communications, I was attending my first media event as the vice president of a large advertising firm. Knowing that John would be in attendance, I spent the afternoon testing witticisms that I planned to sprinkle throughout our conversation. I daydreamed meeting him, feigning to not remember him, then throwing my arms around him and planting a kiss on his cheek. Through tears of joy, I would thank him for turning my life around and for being my Sherpa in the midst of my soul-defining blizzard. We would laugh. Then hug. And perhaps rekindle our friendship.

With sparkling water in hand, I scanned the ballroom. I did not recognize John until he removed his sunglasses. His hair had undergone reverse alchemy from gold to silver. Red and purple spidery veins of the alcoholic breed criss-crossed his cheeks. He looked like he needed a good meal and several days of sleep. He raised his empty martini glass to the waiter who nodded and quickly produced a replacement.

John walked right up to me, swaying noticeably. Alarmed at his appearance and his breath, I took a step back. He came closer and leaned over, his unbuttoned jacket grazing my arm.

"Don't I know you?" he said.

I held my breath.

"Thought you looked like a friend," he said, straightening and putting his sunglasses back on.

With trembling hands, he finished his drink in one swallow and lifted his empty glass to me.

I turned and left him there. That was 11 years ago.

In these past 11 years I have not seen, heard about, talked about, nor thought about John Peel. Consumed with my own life, marriage, children, an MBA, and now starting my own business, I had forgotten all about John until this very moment as I read his obituary in the newspaper.

Searching through my yesteryear phonebook, I found the number for Marcia, an old college friend, who still worked at the Burlington Herald. Marcia answered the phone and spoke to me like we were picking up a conversation left unfinished from yesterday afternoon instead of more than a decade ago. Yes, she had heard about John. Yes it was terrible but not too unexpected. He had been on and off the wagon for most of his life. Had a couple of failed marriages, two or three kids, and finally got fired for good from the newspaper when the drinking got really out of control about eleven years ago. Then he fell off everyone's radar and drifted around until he got sick.

Marcia wanted to know if she would see me at the funeral. I asked if anyone else was going, meaning anyone from the old days. She said that John had touched many lives, and everyone would be in attendance. People would be flying in from all over the country. I made noises about double-checking my schedule and hung up.

John's black and white picture stared at me from the newspaper. I poured myself a shot of my very best cognac and made a toast to John. After drinking it down in one swallow, I poured myself another and sat down to read the obituary again. I replayed our last encounter in my head. He had been in obvious trouble at the time. Even now, I held my breath thinking about that moment when he had come over to talk to me. How I had prayed that he would not recognize me.

My body relaxed, cognac seeping into my muscles and into my mind. I allowed myself to replay our previous interlude from the Christmas party. This one I relived much more slowly, playing the 'what if' game in my head. What if John had kissed me back? What if he hadn't driven me home, but to his place instead? What if he had simply ignored me?

Insight clicked in my head like a million piece puzzle suddenly coming together. John could have easily taken advantage of me with my full blessing. He could have made it even worse by encouraging me to have a few more drinks to blur any memory of the evening. But he blocked my advances even though I knew he wanted to give in; I remember feeling it in his muscles, smelling it on his skin. For the briefest of moments, he had allowed me to kiss him before he held me away. But he did hold me away. He went above and beyond any duty he had towards me, deepening our bond by doing the hard thing, the necessary thing, the right thing. Oh how humiliated I felt. But his words had planted seeds that rooted immediately in my soul. "You are better than this," he said. And it changed my life completely.

Marcia's words swam in my head: his drinking got out of control about eleven years ago. Could I have stopped him? Or could I have made things better? Could I at least have tried? Guilt picked at my insides and I felt the heavy realization that it was too late...too late to rectify, apologize, reciprocate, conciliate.

I poured myself another cognac and played the 'what if' game in my head again. What if I had introduced myself to him at our last meeting, shook his hand and jogged his memory. What if I had said something like: John Peel, I owe you my life, or something like: you're my hero and don't take this the wrong way but I love you. What if I had laughed with him, been kind, taken the drink out of his hand and said let's go get a coffee together? What if? Could I have saved him? Could I have offered life-altering words of wisdom? Could my efforts have been profound? Or impotent? Or something in-between?

Attending the funeral suddenly became a priority. I needed to send expensive flowers, and write a poignant speech to let everyone know that I would not be standing here, a great success in every sense of the word had it not been for John Peel. And I would admit this in front of all those people flying in from all over the country and packing the house because John had touched their lives in some way.

Was this why I hated funerals so much? Not because I was uncomfortable around the idea of death, but because I just did not have any excuses for why I was so damned absent from this person's life. Why did I care enough to send $150 worth of flowers and take a day off work for the funeral, but for over a decade I could not find two minutes to make a phone call and just say hello.

With cognac and regret warming my blood, I lay down on the sofa and imagined white calla-lilies filling the church. And fresh roses draped over a grand brass and mahogany casket. I fell into a thick sleep wondering why friends waited until you were dead before they sent flowers.

So Glad To See You Here
by Gerry Markee

Fifty hunters spread across the ice. They each carried a rifle at the ready and moved with surprising discipline, reminding me of a World War I skirmish line. A hakapik, the infamous seal-killing club, was stuck in their belt. It surprised me. I had always imagined the seal hunters swarming across the ice without plan or purpose, but they were advancing with well-drilled military precision.

A whistle blasted from somewhere on the ice. The hunters came to a stop and fired a volley into the mass of barking seals one hundred yards away. It was easy to see the blood splattered on the pristine snow from the bodies of writhing harp seals. The hunters advanced across the ice. The whistle blasted again. They stopped and fired another volley across the ice. More seals died. Howling and panicked barking rose from the blood-stained ice. The seals panicked, climbing over each other before the advancing hunters.

It was horrible. I thought I was going to be sick. It was an irony not lost on me. I had supported the seal hunt all of my life. Intellectually, it was easy to rationalize the hunt. There were lots of seals, over six million of them, and a quota of only three hundred and fifty thousand. A five percent cull made sense. It made sense until you were on the ice watching it happen. Was it any different than going into an abattoir to watch hamburger being created? It was just that there seemed to be so much blood.

"Lord t'underin', lad. Ye look as white as a harp." Uncle Miles laughed and slapped me on the back.

I took a deep cold breath and then went back into the cabin of the Coast Guard cutter. I lit up a smoke and watched the hunters fire another volley about thirty yards away from the scrambling mass of seals. Maybe I should have stayed in Toronto working as a janitor. It seemed so much more antiseptic and clean than watching the slaughter on the ice.

"Aside lad," said Uncle Miles as he came in and shut the door. He reached up and pulled down the foghorn cord.

The hunters slung their rifles over their shoulders and pulled out their hakapiks. I hardly noticed that. What I noticed were white-clad figures rising from the ice on the other side of the seal herd. Puffs of breath were visible for the first time. The seals were retreating right into the ambush. Where had these guys come from? They charged into the herd with their hakapiks, swiftly dispatching the seals with cold economic strokes of their hakapiks or with pops from their pistols. At the same time, the hunters moved in and joined them in the slaughter.

I looked at Uncle Miles then pointed back over the ice. "Who the hell are those guys?"

Uncle Miles nodded and smiled. "Friends from the old country." The attack lasted over an hour. When it was done, thousands of seals were dead, spread out over the stained ice. There was so much red. Then Uncle Miles sounded the horn again, a long single blast that echoed over the ice sheet of the Front, the largest seal killing ground on the East Coast.

It was good thing we stayed on the cutter. I probably would have lost my breakfast out on the ice. What a disgusting job, staying here and watching the slaughter. The men on the ice were splattered in blood and I could hear their laughing and cheering as they watched the last of the fleeing seals sink into the cold water. Heartless bastards. They began the work of skinning the pelts from the bodies, piling some of the carcasses on the ice and pushing others into the sea.

"What a waste."

Uncle Miles snorted. "Hurumph. 'Tis time for us to go out and check up on things."

We strolled carefully across the ice, but I wished I did not have to go. Still, it would not do to get squeamish now. I had no interest in letting the hunters know how disgusted I was at the sight of the killing. As we slowly made our way across the ice, I began to realize something strange. Those short hunters who had appeared from nowhere were carefully going from body to body in pairs, examining them, but leaving the skinning to the larger hunters. They had no interest in the pelts, but in the seals. When we got closer we got to the site of the slaughter, I realized the strangers were really short guys. At first I thought maybe they were the local Inuit hunters, but since when are Inuit only two feet tall? That could not be right.

"Meagher, what is the count?"

The very short hunter with the silver whistle hanging around his neck stood up and pulled a pack of smokes out of his pocket. "It was a fine day's work, Miles. We took two thousand two hundred and thirty-nine today. Didn't get 'im though." He looked at me, then at Uncle Miles. "Family?"

"This is Mike, son of my brother Jacob. He just moved back to the Rock from Taranna. It's his first time on the ice."

"See the resemblance. Welcome home, Mike. Smoke?" He slid two smokes out of the pack. They looked like hand-rolled joints.

Uncle Miles and I took a smoke and lit up. They weren't joints but the smoke helped. Although I still wanted to be sick, I could not let these guys see that. They would never let me forget it. The East Coasters felt enough contempt for government types already. I wouldn't give them the satisfaction of seeing the city boy fall apart.

"Faith and begorrah, it has been a good day, Miles. We got 'em good." Meagher pulled back his white hood and tugged off his balaclava. He had an old face with a long salt and pepper beard. His arched eyebrows reminded me of Mr. Spock from Star Trek. He even had the pointy ears to match, sort of like a Vulcan in miniature. He thrust out his hand and smiled.

I looked down and shook his hand. I tried to take the smoke out of my mouth, but it stuck to my lip, and my fingers slid along the smoke pulling off the ember with my fingertips. "Damn!" I flicked away the ember but not before it seared my fingers. "He's a leprechaun!"

Uncle Miles smiled. "Of course he is a leprechaun, laddie." Miles shook his head and sighed. "What else would he be?" He turned to the leprechaun. "Excellent work, Meagher."

Meagher looked me over, frowning.. "I can see that Jacob has been a bit remiss in his duties, Miles." He scooped up a bit of snow and pressed it into my fingers. "Be more careful lad." I could only nod. Dad had known about this?

"It happens from time to time," said Uncle Miles.

"I trust you will ensure this is corrected," said Meagher. The leprechaun scratched his beard and smiled. "Listen to your Uncle Miles, laddie. He will set ye straight"

Uncle Miles handed me a clipboard. "Be a good lad and take care of the census. After that we can go home for supper."

I took the clipboard and headed out onto the ice. I went from man to man and marked them off against the list. It sounds easy enough but it wasn't easy to walk through all of those carcasses. Still, I held down my breakfast, important to portray the image of the disinterested Fisheries Officer simply doing his job.

They saw it in my face, I am sure, but these rough men smiled and treated me with respect. I had expected some gags or practical jokes, but it never happened. They acted more like professional soldiers than hunters or fishermen. And then there were the leprechauns.

I had read that leprechauns were flighty little pranksters, but not these guys. They were efficient little soldiers. Each one was armed with a hakapik and a small twenty-two calibre pistol tucked in his belt. It was hard to imagine leprechaun commandoes but they were here and dressed for the part with white seal skin coats and pants.

"O'Flynn, Flaherty, Ryder, O'Halloran ..." I finished the census and returned to the cutter. Meagher was gone, leaving only Uncle Miles in the cabin, smoking and drinking coffee. Uncle Miles handed me a coffee when I handed him the clipboard. I would have preferred a beer, or maybe a good shot of Screech, but Uncle Miles tolerated nothing stronger than coffee on his boat.

He looked over the census and nodded. "Perfect turnout. Excellent. I'll fax this to Ottawa when we get home tonight."

"If you don't mind me being a bit curious; you are going to fax this to Ottawa?"

"Naturally. It's important that the profits are divided properly and that only registered hunters are on the ice. They do expect to get paid after all."

"Leprechauns are registered hunters?"

"Of course. You don't believe that I file false reports with Ottawa?"

"Heaven forbid." I did not know what else to say. This was a little too weird for me. It was easier to imagine Uncle Miles filing an imaginary report than to believe Ottawa was aware of leprechauns clubbing and shooting seals on the ice.

The dories were bobbing softly near the ice when we arrived the next morning. The ice was alive with thousands of seals, squawking and barking, totally oblivious to their fate.

When we were spotted, the hunters pulled up onto the ice and spread out like they had done yesterday. The hunters fired methodical volleys into the seal pack, sending them into a panic. When the seals began to retreat, once again the leprechauns rose from the ice and sprang to the attack. They swept up and around the seal pack cutting off their retreat. Wielding hakapiks and pistols they began the merciless slaughter.

I stood on the bow of the cutter watching the action with my binoculars. I stood by myself for a long time, hardly noticing the cold and dampness until Uncle Miles came to me and handed me the clipboard and census sheets. I went out onto the ice again and counted the same fifty men and fifty leprechauns and recorded over four thousand seals killed. Every day of the seal hunt we sat on our cutter watching the killing and reporting the information to Ottawa at night. I became used to seeing leprechauns killing seals. The only problem for me was getting my head around the idea that Ottawa knew about leprechauns and had obviously known about them for a long time. It made sense to do my job and say nothing. And then the seal hunt ended. We returned to regular patrolling along the coast of Labrador, dropping in to small communities like Black Tickle, Forteau and Mary's Harbour. Some of those towns were smaller than some of the apartment complexes where I had lived in Toronto. All along the coast we drifted by abandoned fishing communities. Uncle Miles knew the names and histories of many of these little ghost villages and spent hours filling my head with tales of crime, government incompetence, and just bad luck.

If you live in Toronto, it is hard to imagine the amount of open space out here. Miles and miles of barren coastlines swept by cold winds and rains in the summer and blistering cold ice and sleet in the winter, it was hard to imagine wanting to live out here, but many had, Vikings, the English, and the Irish. The Vikings were gone but many others still remained. I admired them, while wondering if they were crazy to live in such isolation and deprivation.

We were a few hours out from Makkovik when Uncle Miles took the helm from me and began to coast in to shore. It made me a little nervous to get so close to the rocks, but I had to hope he knew what he was doing. I checked over the maps. "Uncle Miles. This area is pretty shallow"

"Faith and begorrah, laddie, have a little faith. I've been on these waters for over forty years." He pointed inland to slight puffs of smoke rising from unseen buildings.

I stood holding the railings so tight I thought I would bend the steel with my fingers. Uncle Miles weaved his way through the rocks into a small cove that had been sheltered and unseen from the ocean. I had expected another one of those small abandoned villages like so many I had seen before. Instead, there was a sizable village of brightly painted homes, some with picket fences, others with rock fences, but all of them had Canadian flags flying in their front yards. Proud Canadian stores and a tavern called the Maple Shamrock lined the shoreline beside the wharf. I had not seen that many Canadian flags flying since that huge federalist rally during the Quebec referendum of '95. We coasted into the wharf and I finally discovered where the leprechauns had gone when the seal hunt ended. Over two hundred leprechauns lined the wharf waiting for us, cheering and waving little Canadian flags. I wished we got the same reception when we arrived in St. John's. Unfortunately, there were still those who resented being forced to join Canada in 1949. It is nice to be liked.

Uncle Miles stood at the top of the gangplank and waited for Meagher to join him. The old leprechaun strolled up the gangplank puffing on his long pipe. Meagher pulled a flask from his shirt and offered Uncle Miles a drink. It was the first time I had ever seen Uncle Miles drink on duty. He sucked back a long shot and then handed it back to the leprechaun. "Good screech."

"Welcome to Padraig's Cove, laddie," said Meagher with a wide grin. "Everything's in the usual spot?" Miles nodded. Meagher turned to some of his fellows and waved them on board. Four leprechauns bolted up the gangplank and into the hold. Moments later, they came out with four trolleys of boxes wrapped in plastic. The crowd on the wharf cheered and followed the four lads into the tavern.

Miles shook Meagher's hand. "We will see you next month. Everything is all right?"

"Ah faith, Miles. All has been right for a long time. As long as the pot is replenished the future is bright." Meagher vanished from the cutter and followed the crowd into the tavern. There was a strange silence and we were all alone. They had vanished just like they had done on the ice.

Ten minutes later we steered out of Padraig's Cove. I turned to Uncle Miles and sighed. "Okay, okay, I don't get it. The pot is replenished?"

Uncle Miles laughed. "I was wondering when you would crack laddie. They lost their pot of gold long ago. That's why the blessed St. Patrick kicked the thieving seals out of Ireland."

"You mean serpents."

"This is so embarrassing. St. Patrick booted the seals out of Ireland, not the snakes. Who could ever believe cuddly little seals were a threat? They have been searching for the seal's fiendish leader and their gold ever since. We are helping them, a place to live and a little pogie."

"How long have we been helping them?"

"Since 1765. We have been helping our little brothers for a long time."

"1765, eh? And the pot of gold hasn't been found yet?"

Uncle Miles sighed. "It has eluded them for a few centuries. That is why we are out on the ice, lad. And we will stay out on the ice until we have found it." He smiled and shrugged. "I need some coffee. Take the helm lad, and get us to Makkovik before the sun sets." Uncle Miles disappeared down into the galley.

For the first time in my life I had that strange feeling that life made sense. We were championing a seal hunt to help leprechauns get their pot of gold back from evil seals. Until that day, the stars could come and go, the press would make us out to be barbarians, but it would not matter. We would be here.

I stared out at the sea and sighed. It was good to be home.

Lakeside Departure
by Graham J. Ducker

Horace was fagged out. At his age, it was normal to be tired, but this morning - this particular morning - he was feeling downright plumb tuckered out, and the tightness in his chest did not help the situation.

His shaking hand clasped the park bench as he, gasping and wheezing, eased himself onto his bench, which was the one nearest the water fountain. It was also the intersection to the many park paths. It wasn't really 'his' bench, but through time there came to be an unspoken law that reserved that particular spot for Harold.

He had not felt well since the morning when he forced himself out of bed, hurried to the park, there to maintain his daily self-imposed schedule of sitting by the pond from late morning till well into the evening. It was there he enjoyed the comparative peace while watching ducks, geese, pigeons and visitors who were absorbed in their respective worlds.

He berated himself for rushing so but he rationalized that the people *expected* him to be there, there on Harold's Throne.

Many folks knew him by name and enjoyed engaging him in conversations ranging from astrophysics to farming, from genetics to geography. Often the philosophical discussions he inspired made them late for work. They would laugh, hurry off, and vow to return tomorrow to continue the debate.

In his haste, he had forgotten his sandwich, but that was okay because Pete and his food cart would soon be along. Lately, Pete had begun refusing payment saying it was his treat, but Harold insisted upon paying for the ice cream bar. When Pete returned later in the evening, it was the same routine.

Another constant in Harold's life was the Mounted Police Patrol team of Constable Laurie McPherson and Constable James McKinnon who always managed to spend a few minutes with him while their horses drank at the fountain. If it happened to be later than usual, they would escort him home.

Because many major dialogues took place at lunchtime, people often shared their lives as well as their lunches. To them, he was their confidant, their counselor and their grandpa. Although he never told anyone what to do, he easily discerned the root of their problems, and tactfully steered anxious individuals onto corrective courses. There were many evenings, with his heart aching from numerous desperate personal histories, Harold would shuffle off to the boarding house where he would fret all night, hoping he would meet the same anonymous folks in the near future.

The day at the lake followed the same pattern, but today Harold became increasingly edgy and irritated with himself. He found it very difficult to maintain a coherent conversation. People arrived with eager smiles, only to excuse themselves shortly thereafter, and leave with quizzical looks on their faces. When asked if he was all right, Harold, with a wave of his bony hand and his almost toothless smile, assured them he was just very tired today.

He was surprised how late it was when the park lights came on, but told himself that he would just have to wait until the internal heaviness eased up.

Staring out across the pond, Harold smiled weakly as some ducks sliced through the moon's reflection making, he surmised, a perfect image with which to close the day.

He took a deep breath, sighed, and wondered if perhaps a short nap would help.

He did not hear the clip-clop of the horses that stopped in front of him. He did not see the tears from Laurie. He did not hear Constable McKinnon call the coroner's office.

Going Home
by Jake Hogeterp

I have strolled from Sneek's train station into Wilhelmina Park with my ten siblings and their spouses. It's a beautiful sunny day in late May. Holland is at its greenest and most resplendent. Ancient, giant Beech trees stand patient guard just as they did a half-century ago when I was last in this place. Ralph, my oldest brother and now the family patriarch, turns to me and asks, "You were four, right? Do you remember any of this?" "Yes," I say. "Just around the corner there's a pond and a little footbridge..."

It's been nearly a week and half since I arrived in the Netherlands, the country of my birth, but I have not yet found a connection. Maybe it was the dull grey-green flatness that first loomed out of the mist on our approach to Schiphol Airport. Or it may have been the shock of the familiar as we sped by acres and acres of steel-clad factories the efficient airport shuttle could not get us by quickly enough. Something about those first impressions shattered my anticipation of the blemish-free postcard perfection I had cherished all these years. Even old Amsterdam required instant revision, all its lore and lure suddenly evaporating as the rawness of a city in its mid-morning bustle casually ignored yet another horde of tourists freshly disgorged from Central Station.

Not that we were daunted – Tara, my daughter and I. Like the veteran troupers we fancied ourselves, we soon doused our jetlag with a few Heinekens in the very building that wondrous brew was first drawn. And we did the art galleries – the Rijksmuseum with its excess of somber burghers staring at us from oversized canvases and foreign centuries, leaving us dazed; the too many abstractions in the van Gough Museum giving us eyestrain. What were they thinking when they slapped up that incongruous shoebox?

What were they thinking when they hid Anne Frank's house behind that dreadful post-modern façade? Maybe that the visitor needs to be eased into this nightmare, requires a barrier between now and then, between what was and still could be.

Even so it was not enough to shield me from a paralyzing wave of emotion when confronted with her portrait at the narrow entrance to the stark hideaway. Forever she gazes past the camera and over the heads of her visitors, gracing them with that beguiling half smile, certain of a return to happier times, any day now.

The playbill of the Concertgebouw featuring Beethoven's sixth briefly lifted my spirits. "Wow, the symphony with which I danced you around the living room when you were little – the one with the rowdy picnic and the storm, and the marvelous peaceful calm after the storm – remember?" To her credit she did, though her tastes have since digressed. Alas the performance was sold out. We had to content ourselves with admiring the hall's peculiar fusion of faux Greek and functional Dutch architecture from a bench across the street.

Mixing it up with the big city locals proved less intimidating than I had feared. Culture shock, though: a corner pub where strangers actually mingled! Maybe it was the tight space, or it could as easily have been the Middle Earth homeliness of the décor. Whichever, once we discovered that a moderately loosened tongue if employed with restraint, could buy a little harmless notoriety, we were in. It didn't take our host long to draw us into his orbit, once he'd graciously dismissed an Irish tourist whose blarney had exceeded house decorum. We got through the where-are-you-from in a fine blend of fractured Dutch and slurred English, much to the merriment of the regulars. I was beginning to congratulate myself on the exotic aura I must be exuding ("... *first time back in 52 years!*"), when he let out that he himself was from Turkey, and had also lived in Montreal for a few years. "Welcome home," he announced at last, handing me a shot of Jenever – the pungent, official drink of Dutch hospitality – on the house, of course. I had visions of assembled uncles in those lean times having scraped their pennies together for a half litre to send my father off. Surplus, we were, expendable, only to be replaced by 'guest labourers' recruited from all corners of the globe a decade later, as the country's prospects improved. 'Cheers', I wanted to say. 'Thanks for standing in'. But I was still able to manage some self-control.

I'm not sure how we got Tara pulling taps, but she took to it like a seasoned pro. She especially liked the tongue depressor-like stick used for striking the foam off the top of the glass. She wielded it like a wand, enchanting the patrons. The bartender left her to it, confident that she, though lacking one of the official languages, could manage capably. In fact he summoned a couple glasses himself, and handing me one, toasted my homecoming once again – only this time he meant it as in 'permanent'. "I've been to Toronto," he said. "If you insist on staying in Canada..." (He must have noticed my demurring, noncommittal smile). "... at least move to Montreal – so much more class. But look, your lovely daughter has a job here already. This is where you really belong!" A moment later, while he wasn't looking, I signalled Tara a wrap up sign. It was time to go.

I needed to shake off the city for a while. A landscape fix, some kind of pastoral retreat, was called for. Rented bicycles to the rescue. We pedalled along a linden–bowered dike that stretched for miles along a wide canal. Self-powered barges churned up and down the quiet water. The aft sections looked as if cozy little places from the suburbs were floating by, complete with requisite car in the driveway. And on our right, quaint cottages and meadows with cattle and sheep grazing soundlessly – Dutch Masters scenery come-to-life. Here and there a smoke stack or a high-rise, remnants of the receding city, poked through the horizon. But the illusion mostly held. Even the ice cream cart at the mid-point, being equal parts intrusion and relief, didn't break the spell.

Since she had only a week and wanted to see as much of the country as she could in that limited time, Tara had suggested an excursion by train to Maastricht, the Netherlands' oldest and southernmost city. The train, uninhibited by any variation in grade, sped along without effort. After pointing out an occasional windmill, and the thatched roofs of a couple of farmsteads, I soon tired of seeing grass as green on one side as on the other. We each retreated to our own fiction discretely stashed for just such insurance.

The guidebooks had not failed Tara. Maastricht lived up to its post card billing – a picturesque outpost that had absorbed the relentless upheavals of its long history. And there were hills. At least in the distance there was a hint of the more solid mainland Europe. Church towers and ancient fortifications dominated the skyline. The red tower of the Saint Jan church stood out among these. Here was a landmark that drew us by its simple, yet elegant design and by its unique colouration. We paid our couple of Euros to the church volunteer committee and climbed the winding stone stairs. As we emerged on the parapet, I noticed that the brick was peeling like blistered paint. I discretely plucked a large flake and watched it flutter to the ground, perversely pondering the Tahiti butterfly wing flap and Kansas tornado effect. Was my tiny act of vandalism hastening the day when all this once-glorious splendour would crumble to irretrievable dust?

Our week was up. I had to leave Tara to find her way back to the airport and to continue alone, to Friesland, my native province, and eventually to Sneek, the city I'd first called home. The train to Friesland made several stops in cities I knew only by name - Amersfoort, Harderwijk, Zwolle. It clattered through more flat, green country that took over abruptly where the urban architecture ended. I wanted so much to know the precise moment we entered Friesland, but there were no signs posted, nor any clues from the landscape. My fellow passengers seemed utterly indifferent to our progress, and I wondered if they, chatting mostly in Dutch, felt any sense of foreignness as we finally pulled into the Leuwarden station.

I needed refreshment before catching the final connection. At the snack bar a young woman was engaging a customer in a lively exchange in the Friesian language. I felt a jolt of elation. Yes, I was indeed in Friesland! But her colleague, older and ever so dour, completed her perfunctory transactions in a monotone Dutch. When she asked what I would like, I couldn't muster a single Friesian phrase and managed only to stammer something in broken English about a single-scoop vanilla.

At a smaller platform, away from the main terminus, I spotted the little local train that would take me the rest of the way. As I stepped aboard, I knew for certain that my dream of travelling through Friesland was finally a reality. But when we got rolling, all I could see was the same green flatness I'd seen everywhere else. I was still a stranger travelling through a foreign landscape that didn't fit with family lore. Even as we approached Sneek, first a newer suburb and then the main station, nothing matched the memories I had carried all these years. I was glad that we had chosen Warkum, the next stop, as the base for our reunion. Sneek would have to wait until I was ready for it.

Several school kids got off the train as I did. They dashed to the bike racks and raced homeward, carefree as a flock of birds. I dragged my luggage from the train stop in search of our hotel somewhere at the far end of town. The tiny wheels were in danger of disintegrating as they clattered over the cobblestones. Having no idea where I was headed, I stopped to ask for directions at a service station. This time the mother tongue served me well, and I may even have passed for a disoriented local.

I hoped that the assembled kin would somehow ground me in this land from which the family tree had so long ago been uprooted. But when I finally reached the beautifully converted farmstead that would be our home for the next week, I found everyone too busy with settling-in and with worry about the late arrivals, to take much notice of any anxiety I might be feeling. Not even the welcoming visit from cousin Henk with his unique gut-splitting humour delivered in the nearly extinct Sneek dialect could pull me out of the funk in which I was mired.

"...That's right," says Ralph, beaming with joy at the shared memory.

As we round the bend, I am suddenly taken aback by the scene before me. The pond, the ducks, the riotous colour of flowers whose names I have never learned – they're all still there. Time has stopped. *It's 1952 again. My brothers and sisters are initiating me in a game of racing around the pond. I hold Ralph, the starter's right hand; my sister Alice, his left. His ready-set-go, peculiar to this game, echoes like a schoolyard mantra. "Vuur! Vlam! Los!" he shouts, priest-like, vigorously pumping our arms with each syllable as he invokes fire and flame to send us off. Alice and I dash off in opposite directions, tearing around the pond, nearly colliding at the mid point on the bridge, each determined to be the first to grasp the outstretched arm the other just relinquished.*

I have found my patch of holy ground. In this place memory and family myth congeal. I sense that I too, finally have a stake in the adventure that was abruptly halted when our sudden emigration tore us from this idyllic paradise. I now know why my later improvisations of this game – around the many houses we valiantly called home, or even once around an improvised baseball diamond – never caught on or satisfied.

This ritual belongs here, as does a part of myself – a part that I hope my family will some day help me reclaim.

The Oolit Tales
by John Jansen in de Wal

Mighty Maud

Mighty Maud was the biggest woman in all of Indiana.
She stood seven feet nine inches. She weighed nobody-knew-how-much. When a young teenager, Skinny Nat teased this farmer's daughter into getting on the town's cattle scale. The scale collapsed under Maud's mass. She never went on it gain. But, skinny Nat teased and ridiculed her every chance he had. He called her names whenever he had the opportunity; names like Fatso, Big Boob, Big Buns, Lardo and a host of others.

Nat also played mean little tricks on her wherever he went. But the two tricks he never repeated were these; putting tacks on the ground where Maud used to sit in the shade of the old oak. She never seemed to feel it, and so there was no fun in it. The other was throwing burrs in her hair. When Maud tried to take them out that first time, she became frustrated and cut her hair so short, burrs would not stick anymore.

But he did tie her shoe laces together when she slept in her resting place. He did throw burrs on the back of her lumberjack shirt or, when she walked in her finery, on her dress, and Maud had to spend hours taking them off.

Now, the day Maud broke the scale, she had laughed in the most hearty and infectious manner. A laugh so inspiring, the dairy herds for miles around filled their udders to bursting. Their owners had hurriedly milked for several hours that late afternoon and wagonloads of butter were churned from the plentiful flow of that day. Maud however had just gone on with her life, ignoring Skinny Nat's taunts, though she was tempted at times.

Now, Maud was not just big, as in tall. No, she was big in girth too. The mighty ham hocks of her hands enabled her to milk her father's cows two at a time. The flip and flop of the flesh under her upper arms was deceptive. When she lifted the bales of hay, three at a time, from the loft into the barn, her biceps swelled larger than the shanks of the family's team of Belgians.

Maud always smiled. She had an infectious glimmer in her eyes. Everywhere she went people could not help but smile with her. The beautiful white teeth that glistened between her rosy lips were a major part of her bigness. They sparkled large even when the sun did not shine. Maud's head was larger than the prize turnip of her sixteenth year. It sat huge and proud atop the firm lines of her broad shoulders.

Maud's bosom outsized the best milking cows' udders in Oolit County. She had long since outgrown the sturdy, well baleened triple-D brazier of her seventeenth birthday. Even when she was not hard at work, the mighty rift between those two mellow mountains forever glistened with the stream of perspiration that filled their deep valley.

Maud's lower torso would not be denied its honourable part in her bigness. Like a huge pear, her bulging hips, comparable in size to the hefty mammaries that filled her over-shoulder-boulder- holder to overflowing, bulged in the space of her too tight 10-X jeans. Wherever she sat down, they left their mighty imprint. That is how the stump of the big old oak at the south east corner of Oolit County's major intersection had become somewhat of a tourist attraction.

It had happened one early spring. A tornado, more powerful than even one hundred and eleven year old Josh could remember, had brought down the aged oak.

Its roots had been tilted up on one side with the force of the wind. It had however refused to fall all the way, and so the tree had leaned across the road enough to keep people from travelling. Out of respect for a tree that had stood since before pioneer days, and because Mighty Maud had always stopped to sit and rest under it, the county fathers had the trunk cut on an angle to form an oval seat for Maud to sit on. When Maud inaugurated her special throne, the imprint of her mighty thighs and buttocks sank deep into the still soft grain of the wood and so there were now two prints of Mighty Maud's pear, the one on the ground and the one on the stump.

Now, Maud's solid-like-a-tree-trunk-legs walked in size thirty three boots. And though she created large holes for puddles when it rained and minor dust devils when it was hot and dry, they moved nimbly wherever Mighty Maud went.

Mighty Maud was huge in circumference of shoulder, chest, hip, thigh, calf and foot as well as stature, but people loved her most for her big-heartedness. Maud, you see, was kind. She loved the birds and the bees, the beautiful petals of all the field flowers; yes, even the weeds, and she cared for her father's cattle and horses. She fed the pigs with gusto, dreading the day they had to be slaughtered for her to eat.

People said that it was no wonder that Maud should be so gentle and kind. In such a huge body there just had to be a sizable heart. And the people were right. Mighty Maud had a big heart: a heart full of love and caring; a heart filled with all the goodness of mother's milk, which was amply evidenced by what she carried in front of it; a heart bursting with a joy and happiness that put a permanent smile on her glorious countenance.

But, then came the day, burned into people's memories, its events told and retold forever since, that Mighty Maud's happy smile must have darkened. Must have, even if for only a very short moment, but darkened nevertheless, and everybody swore to it. It was the day Skinny Nat fell down the steep cliffs that surrounded Splat Pond on all sides.

***

Now, Splat Pond was a deep, deep hole in the ground at the southern boundary of Oolit County. The water in it was far down. The sides were so steep, nobody had ever gone down them for fear they might not be able to climb back up. And so nobody knew how deep Splat Pond really was. And that is why nobody ever climbed or jumped down those cliffs to swim there.

But, to get back to Skinny Nat, he had been doing his usual teasing of Mighty Maud as she walked one Summer Sunday in her finest along the field road that skirted the edge of Splat Pond. He had been throwing burrs, pebbles and small clumps of dry clay at her while following her at a short distance. For just once Maud decided to do something about it. She turned around and said "Boo".

Now, nobody knows whether it was the unexpected retaliation or the sudden eruption of air with which that 'Boo' came out of Maud's mighty lungs, but Skinny Nat fell off the cliff and into the depth of Splat Pond.

Maud was shocked. She froze to the ground where she stood, paralyzed like a solid mountain. She felt she had to rescue Nat, but her fear of water caused her to waver. She remembered the day of her fifth birthday when she nearly drowned in Oolit Creek. She had joined the other kids in an afternoon swim. But her petticoats and dress had soaked up so much water that they weighed her down to the point where she could not get up. Nor had her friends been able to pull her to safety. It had taken three farm hands who were ploughing nearby to get her out with their teams of horses.

That is why Maud understood the fear that resonated in Nat's screams: the shrillest screams ever heard in Oolit County, the echoes off which bounced off the six foot high, steep walls surrounding him as he tumbled. And as they reached out of the hollow that held the pond, they blared like a trumpet not only over Oolit but also the neighbouring counties. And as the echoes kept bouncing and blaring, people ran to the pond from all over.

Maud meanwhile did the only thing she could. She decided to save Nat. To be sure she would not drown, she removed her many petty coats and other accouterments.

And so it was that the first men to run up the field road, were treated to a sight never before seen nor ever after observed. The milky white body of Mighty Maud sailed through the air toward the surface of Splat Pond that rippled with Skinny Nat's desperate flailing to stay afloat.

What happened next would be unbelievable were it not for the fact that every single citizen of Oolit County, and many from the surrounding area, even if they had not been there, are to this day, willing to swear to it on an assorted stack of bibles and other holy books.

When the well endowed body of big hearted Maud hit the water in an attempt to save the one who had been so nasty to her for so many years, the splash that resulted drove all the water up the six foot cliff, baptizing one and sundry who had come near. And as they recovered from the shock and wiped their faces, they saw Mighty Maud's smiling countenance appearing over the edge of the cliff. She laid Skinny Nat dripping and all in the dust of the field road. Turned out, Splat Pond had less than a foot of water in it.

Well, when Maud climbed out, the sight of her Mightiness filled all the many eyes of Oolit County's populace and then some. And it pained those eyes so much that not just the women, but even the men could not handle the sight, and had to turn their heads.

And if you ever come to Oolit County in the Indiana of these United States, you will see a third mighty imprint of Mighty Maud's pear at the bottom Splat Pond.

Hinkel Pinkel

Now, local legend has it that the pond was formed when a one-legged giant from Baltimore, Maryland hopped by on his way to the West. The existence of a string of similar ponds at reasonably similar distances along a more or less straight line to Wichita, Kansas lends credence to the tale.

The Oolit County tellers of the tale of Hinkel Pinkel speak of a young giant who was unhappy with his lot by the sea. He could not go fishing because all the boats were too small for him. And so Hinkel Pinkel had to stay home.

Hinkel Pinkel decided to fish in the bay. He would stand hip deep in the water and toss a net. When he discovered he could catch fish with his bare hands he abandoned his net. Bare hand fishing was much more fun.

All went well till the day he got into a vicious fight with the biggest shark ever seen before or since in Chesapeake Bay. Hinkel Pinkel had caught a baby shark with his hands that day. The mama shark obviously did not like that and bit his lower left leg right off, something like; you take my baby, I take your leg.

Anyway, after many months of healing of the stump of his left leg, Hinkel Pinkel was able to begin learning to walk. But he was impatient and found that it was easier to hop on one leg then to try walking with one leg and the stump of a leg. And in time, Hinkel Pinkel became the best hopper ever and won every one-legged race at every sports event up and down the coast.

Eventually Hinkel did not find fun in these events any more. He needed a greater challenge, and since nobody knew how to give him one, he thought of one himself. He had heard about runners crossing the continent, one faster than the other. Most on horse, but some on foot as well. And so Hinkel decided to be the first to cross the continent hopping on one leg and set a continental hop record that would last for many a year. He would leave Maryland, hop on over The Great Mississip, through the Nevada Desert, and in one huge bound right across the Grand Canyon and over the mountains to the California coast.

But, as with many man-made plans, Hinkel Pinkel's too came to naught. He was very successful for the first part of his venture. He managed a fast time right up to the Mighty Mississip. He had not thought he would tire on his quest. But he did. He made the river leap and landed barely with his heels on the western bank of that mighty river. Determined to succeed, he renewed his every effort, leaving deep holes wherever he landed.

Then it began to rain. Hinkel Pinkel started to slip each time he hopped, till, suddenly, just when his huge body zoomed through the air as it crossed the border between Kansas and Colourado, he fell.

Now, that is where the story of Hinkel Pinkel ends. No matter who tells it, that is all any Oolit County teller of this tale knows. People think it is because the end of the tale lies somewhere far to the west and is not really of any consequence to them.

Still they tell what they know because it is their way of honouring the memory of Hinkel Pinkel who gave them Splat Pond. And, yes, a good tale helps pass the time on a sultry summer day when they sit rocking their chairs on the shaded front porch regaling gullible tourists.

Should I Stay or Should I Go
by Kathy Buckworth

As I sit in my kitchen and watch my five year old daughter Bridget load her Ken doll into the car while Barbie waves goodbye from the comfort of her Dream House, I suggest that perhaps the Mommy/Barbie could go to work instead. She laughs "Yeah. I'm sure Mommies go to work." So there it is: my twenty year career gone, poof, erased in just over two years with a wave of Barbie's tiny fused plastic hand.

Stay At Home. Go To Work. Door Number One or Door Number Two. Where is Monty Hall when you need him? As a mother of four young children I probably have the egg in my purse. But this is not a game. This is real life.

When faced with a difficult choice, I select the option that fills me with the most relief. For years my relief choice was Go. Go. Go. We all have belief systems which remain fairly static through our lives. I discovered however that my *relief system* could change. And did. One day, standing in my apocalyptic front hall, briefcase strap slung over my shoulder, chewed fingernail pointing harshly to my overflowing daytimer, I explained to my daughter that I couldn't possibly purchase new gym shoes for her until a week from Tuesday. How had I gotten into this position, and was it where I wanted to be? Then It happened. The choice to Stay became my relief. Mostly...

Stay. What is it about that word that is negative? Stay At Home Mom. No, just Stay. Don't Go. Stay At Work Mom – this isn't used. Why? I have to Go to work. I can't Stay at home. All right then, just Go. Go is moving forward, getting out, doing something. Staying is somehow settling. And settling must somehow be bad.

Now women are either blessed or cursed with the option of choice. Stay At Home. Fine if you have kids. Bad and lazy if you do not. Go to work. Fine if you don't have kids. Bad and cold hearted if you do. If I Stay at work too late, I could be rewarded with praise and compliments from the type of people I don't want to be friends with. If I Go home too early, I will be faced with contempt from the same. Going to work is hard when you have children. Staying at home with them is not easy.

Are women who Stay at home with their children performing a selfish or unselfish act? Are they depriving their household of needed income and indulging themselves in a romantic version of the family ideal? Are the women who Go to work ignoring their family and taking a job from someone who needs it, particularly when most of her income goes to pay for daycare services for her children? Is she only satisfying her own needs at the expense of others?

Do men want to have the same choices? Women are further ahead in the choice lottery but further behind in the expectations sweepstakes. If I choose to stay at home, and by doing so, leave a good job, does that indicate to others that I am avoiding work, or that my once fabulous career is not so?

If I try to at least slow things down and admit to my boss that I am not interested in seeking a promotion, am I really bringing my career to a grinding halt, earning bad reviews, and then moving myself to a decision to leave work? You can't Stay when you're at work; you have to be constantly moving upwards and onwards. Like a shark that stops swimming, if you stop reaching, it will be out of reach.

When you work full time you have mixed emotions about the women you know who had made a choice to stay at home. Some had gladly given up their less than stellar careers, perhaps unintentionally signalling that this had been part of the master plan. Some haven't "worked" for years; their children now mostly grown and out of the house all day with school and other pursuits, yet they remain. They Stay. In the house. Why? You envy some of them, have disdain for others, and complete condescension with whom you feel the most competition. What kind of a stay at home mother is respected or acceptable? Do I want to be that sweat pant wearing overweight slob obsessed only with my child and not my own ambitions and appearance? Do I want to be that aerobic Mom and leave my children (whom I left work to be with), in the care of others whose job it is to take care of my children, while their own are being cared for by someone else? How do I find the hallowed middle ground?

Am I allowed to spend money if I haven't earned the money myself? How much? On what? Is there always guilt?

Should there be any? Can money grow on trees? Ah well I don't garden either.

Should the house be clean? Should I be the one cleaning it? Can I pay someone to clean my house when no one pays me to do anything, because I just Stay? At Home.

Who are these other people I see during the day when they should be Going to work? Are they Staying around for a certain reason? Are they unemployed losers or mothers without jobs? Is there a difference?

Why don't men have these thoughts? Do they have these thoughts? Why is it that there is nothing manly about Dad who Stays. Dad's who stray get more approval than Dads who Stay. Their wives are overbearing, overambitious bitches, and they are lazy, stupid, and suspect.

Do the children need me? Do they want me? Do they notice me? Do I care? Am I a bad Stay at home mother because I can go long periods of time without wanting to see them? The sense that I have filled up the time chart with "time spent with children" as if it were another item on my invisible and meaningless "to do" list (right next to "empty dishwasher" and "contemplate dinner")

Is it good to have time to think? Isn't better not to over think things, and just do? Why do I think about things like this?

Do I have to drive a van? Can't I have a normal adult car, or is that trying to eradicate the fact that I have children and re-live a youth that never was. Do I have to drive the damn van every day, to every place that they want to go? Is that part of the job? Why don't people get paid for providing basic services? Why don't children get paid by the government so that they in turn can pay their mothers to Stay? Just Stay.

If, as a working mother, the children frustrate you between the hours of 6:30 and 9:00 at night and during weekends, isn't the expectation that this will in some way subside ridiculous? If you felt underappreciated in your efforts to feed and clothe your children when you were part-timing it with them, get ready to feel like a piece of furniture or machinery in full-time mode.

Is this what women have achieved after fifty years of fighting for equality? It's come down to two choices which have developed such strong stereotypical personalities, defined mostly by us. The Women. When you are that mother with a career you enjoy and want to hold on to, why does it say that you don't particularly like and want to hold on to your children as well?

The two main disadvantages of staying at home to be with your children are that you are expected to a) Stay at Home, and b) Be With Your Children. To be perfectly clear, when you Stay At Home, you are technically allowed to leave the house. You may venture out to the schools, the hockey arenas, the houses of your children's friends (for that ridiculously termed "playdate"), and other convenient areas where children are known to congregate. They do like to be amongst their own type. You will take your mini-van. This is done. You may also leave the children in the care of others (teachers, relatives, husbands, friends) in a pathetic attempt to continue with the social life you fostered while working. This is hard. The old crowd may feel betrayed or puzzled by your new path. They will attempt to unearth the "real" reason for this diversion. Particularly the working mothers themselves who are still looking for the Holy Grail which leads to the right choice between Stay or Go.

You will be asked and also told about your time at home with the children. "So, you're at home with the children?" (Condescension level adjustable.) Resist the urge to answer "*No I'm standing right in front of you, you idiot.*" As their eyes search frantically for someone more worthy to speak to once the word "Yes" pops out of your mouth, you have several options for a quick completion of the sentence. "*Yes I am and I love every minute of it!*" (I.e. you're kind of a lying freak and you will be speaking to air momentarily.) "*Yes and its the hardest job I've ever done*", (i.e. you've clearly never had a real job outside your house and are also certainly the type of person to follow that up with "*I don't know when I had time to work!*" And clearly, you didn't. They will stop for the obligatory snort of derision.) "*Yes-I-gave-up-my-high-powered-career-to-allow-my-husband-and-I-to-enjoy-a-better-lifestyle*" (said without drawing breath; be prepared to provide real-life examples of this "better lifestyle" which can hold them for a few minutes.) These are the same people who didn't care to ask about your professional life when you had one. Particularly the men. They didn't want to know then, and they're just proving something now.

***

After the births of my first 3 children, I couldn't wait to get out of The House and back to The Office. Slavery to the commute and the schedule, but freedom from the drudgery and the boredom. And where is my coffee? That coffee that someone else has made and will allow me to purchase from them without struggling with squalling infants, bothersome toddlers and errant pre-schoolers.

I can still see my eldest daughter Victoria (then aged 8) standing in our driveway at 6:45 a.m. on a cold dark winter's morning, with me physically prodding her with my briefcase along to the car in order to deposit her and her brother at the daycare right at opening time. She turned to me, tears running down her face and said "Mom, why do you work?" I had about four seconds to come with an answer which would encompass the virtue of striving for accomplishment, while not degrading the many stay at home Moms she knew in her neighbourhood, and justified the worthwhile sacrifice of spending more time with her and her younger brother. Before I could spit it out, her world wise 6 year old brother Alexander answered simply "Vicky, she only does it for the money".

I acquiesce just slightly that this certainly is a motivator, as well as a guarantor to holidays, treats, and toys. As I begin to pontificate more passionately about achievement, self-worth and intellectual stimulation it is only to be shut down by the rebuttal question of "Doesn't Daddy make enough money?", followed up immediately by the sucker punch of "Do my friends' Daddies make more money so that their Moms can stay at home with them?" and the killer blow "Are their Moms not smart enough to work?" No, No, and YES! I scream silently. And so we go on.

"Why do you like meetings better than you like me?" Says Alexander. Twist the knife just a little bit more. And sometimes I do. Like the meetings that is. Although lately not so much. The inaneness of the newest long term strategies (Economies of Enthusiasm; Ready, Aim, Win; Customer-centric Vision; Self-flagellation Steps to Success) coupled with the "same shit, different day"

I didn't feel like a cold hearted bitch, it wasn't all about the money but it was mine and I had earned it. I had a right to it. How and when did the creeping guilt become so powerful?

***

Here's the way I see it. After years of post-secondary education, twenty years in the workforce, slowly but successfully winding my way to a highly paid, respectable position, while

138

juggling four pregnancies resulting in four children and its assorted accoutrements...and it's all come down to two options. One: I can carry on working and perpetuate the image of the cold hearted bitch, the uncaring parent, the selfish cow, while I take a man's rightful job because my husband falls short in some meaningful way. Did I mention I'm an uncaring parent? (But I get to drive the BMW and read the paper uninterrupted.) Or, Two: I can stay at home with the children which will tell everyone that I am unable to find a real job, I'm lazy, subordinate to my husband, a shameless free-loader and an overprotective psycho who doesn't trust her children with anyone else during the day. (But I don't have to leap out of bed at the sound of a screaming alarm, pull together clothes that make a statement, listen to pontificating assholes, or worry about the school buses being cancelled.) Choice is freedom. Freedom is choice. Now Choose.

Growing Up at the Cottage
A memoir by Liisa Hypponen

Every year after school ended in June, my parents would pack my brothers and me into the family's 1955 gray Buick with the white-wall tires and red interior, and we'd travel north on Highway 2 towards our cottage at Canning Lake. Along our route we'd stop at the takeout window in Coboconk for French fries smothered in vinegar, salt and ketchup in cardboard containers. Then we'd continue on our way. Nestled in the back seat, I'd sleepily wait for the sound of our tires crunching on gravel, the signal that we were pulling into the parking lot of Joe Plut's 24-hour convenience store with the crooked sign announcing, "We doze but never close." My mother would load her arms with groceries, while my brother and I grabbed Archie comic books and bags full of three-for-a-penny blackballs. Five minutes later, the car would turn off the highway onto a rough dirt road at the edge of the forest. We'd bump along through the woods, then past the farmer's fields with the lounging black and white cows. My brother or I would let out a loud moo, and we'd laugh hysterically. Finally we'd arrive.

Our pine cottage, built by my grandfather from the trees on the land, sat upon a platform of rock overlooking the lake. Everywhere white birch and evergreens rose high. Patches of fern and trilliums blanketed the ground. All weekend long the cottage hummed with the activity of my grandparents, mother, father, aunt, uncle, baby brother Jack, big brother Rob, Cousin Tim and his nasty sister Maggie. We'd sauna, swim, pick berries, run in the woods, read comics, suck blackballs, and late at night, after roasting marshmallows over an open fire, or an endless game of Monopoly 'round the pine dining table, we'd fall exhausted into our bunks. I didn't sleep right away, but would lay in the comfort of my bed listening to the cry of the loons on the lake while staring out the window into the blackness imagining what evils hid in the dark.

As idyllic a place as our cottage was, spending time there had its dramatic moments. Situations arose every once in a while that had to be dealt with. There was the time our dog Brownie, a

Boxer, came home from a run in the woods with her snout full of porcupine quills. Hastily we loaded the dog, somewhat stunned by its misfortune, into the Buick and drove her to the vet in Lindsay to have the needles pulled out—one by one. You'd think after that harrowing experience the dog would have had the sense to steer clear of the prickly creature, but no, on two more occasions we repeated the same trip.

Then there was the time we had to rescue my grandfather from his fishing mishap. He liked to go out on the lake, a short distance from shore, with his tackle and gear in the small aluminium rowboat to try his luck. My granddad would row the shiny boat out a couple of hundred feet, drop the anchor, and cast his fishing line. One afternoon a group of us basking in the sun after a swim watched him from the dock. He cast his line and within a few minutes the buoy attached to it started to burble in the water. A fish had obviously caught the hook. Grandpa, with a grin on his face, vigorously began to reel in his catch. In his fisherman's excitement he turned quickly, lost his footing, swayed to one side and then it happened—man overboard.

All of us leapt to our feet shouting, "He fell in. Grandpa fell in the lake." My dad rushed out from the boathouse, jumped into our small motorboat tied to the dock, and accompanied by my brother Rob, quickly made his way to the floundering man. They managed to pull him aboard, tie a rope to the aluminum dinghy and bring both man and boat safely ashore. Somehow, in all the commotion, my grandfather had saved the fish, and we all enjoyed a fresh catch of the day at dinner that night, along with a good laugh at my granddad's expense.

Whenever these misadventures happened, I secretly wished the victims were my big brother Rob or cousin Maggie. Those two liked to spend a lot of their time tormenting me.

They'd hold me hostage in the boathouse on a regular basis, telling me all sorts of grizzly tales. There were big bears in the woods, they said, that came after little girls, especially those that wandered the forest alone, something I did nearly every day. Eventually, they'd free me from their capture, and I'd run swiftly up the path to the cottage before one of the brown beasts got to me. Another of their mean pranks, I remember, happened on one of our berry-picking ventures. My grandmother would give us plastic containers and send us up the hill to fill them with raspberries and blueberries that she'd put in her scrumptious pies when baking. Of course, we popped a few of the juicy morsels into our mouths as we picked. One day Rob and Maggie told me I'd eaten some poison berries and then went into a detailed description of the horrible bellyache I would soon experience. All the way home I waited for the pain to strike. I walked behind them fearing my ultimate death until we arrived back at the cottage, and my mother, seeing my distress, reassured me that raspberries and blueberries aren't poisonous. The two had a big laugh over that one.

When my folks were around, Rob and Maggie didn't bother me too much, but on Sunday night, my mother and father drove back to the city and left us kids with our grandparents for the week. It was then I really had to beware.

I loved my cottage days when I wasn't being tormented by those two. I spent my time floating on inner tubes in the lake, or flying high on the wooden swing suspended from ropes slung over the branches above. Sometimes I'd sway back and forth in my grandpa's rocker singing along to Chantilly Lace or Peggy Sue on the radio. Other times I'd wander through the forest for hours. There wasn't much in the woods that frightened me except the thought of a surprise visit from rotten Rob and mean Maggie, as I liked to call them. Occasionally I'd hear a rustling in the trees and grow wary wondering if they lurked close by. I used to think I'd prefer an unexpected encounter with a king-size Sasquatch over an ambush by those two. Whenever they did catch sight of me they would chase me through the woods until I'd flee to the safe haven of my nana's kitchen where she'd be cooking by the big black stove with the fire inside.

One sunny afternoon I was leaping from rock to rock at the water's edge when I heard the sound of trampling feet and rotten Rob and mean Maggie yelling, "Let's get her!"

My heart began to pound as I planned my escape. In my panic, I slipped on a rock and toppled into the drink. Coughing and sputtering, I spat out the mouthful of lake I had swallowed and quickly climbed to the shore. The two were fast approaching. I ran with all my might, soaking wet and screaming, along the path, and up the hill, leaving the bullies far behind. I burst through the cottage door, past my nana at the big black stove and into my room. I sat nervously on the edge of my bunk, trying to catch my breath. I must have been there for ten minutes when I again heard cries and screeching and the pounding of feet. Rob and Maggie exploded through the cottage door, crying, "The bees, the bees, they've stung us!"

"Oh what good fortune," I thought as I stood with my ear to the wall. I muffled my gleeful snickering as my weeping tormentors told my nana of how they fell into a hornets' nest while playing in the woods, and the beasts came after them. Their cries faded as my grandmother led them to the medicine chest to administer some first aid.

The rest of the afternoon wore off quietly. I dried myself from my plunge in the lake, put on fresh clothes, picked out a book to read and lay on my bunk. I wondered, as I drifted off to sleep, why Rob and Maggie liked to bug me so much. Maybe it was because I often had my nose in a book, or perhaps they found me rather precocious, as had my mother. But really, I think they did it just because they could. I was no match for the two of them. After all, I was only six years old. They were much bigger and craftier at ten.

At dinnertime my grandmother woke me. I had slept for three hours exhausted from the events of the afternoon. I joined the others around the gleaming pine table to devour one of my nana's delicious meals. She had been cooking and baking most of the afternoon. There was not the usual talk and banter at supper that night. Rob and Maggie remained silent when my grandmother placed a platter of chicken and potatoes before us, then removed her glasses and examined their swollen cheeks before she took her seat. I must admit I felt quite pleased as I gazed across the table at Rob and Maggie, my oppressors, their glum faces spotted with pink calamine to ease the itch of the stings that covered them.

I guess the two of them learned their lesson that afternoon. They never bothered me much again, but they sure did scurry away every time a bee buzzed their way. As for me, the next year at school I placed first in the 100-yard dash at the track meet. It must have been all that training I had over the summer, running through the woods.

Ten Loaves of Bread
by Margo Georgakis

"Take him a gift of ten loaves of bread, some cakes, and a jar of honey, and ask him what will happen to the boy."- 1 Kings 14:3 ...

Rap. Rap. Rap. A shotgun banged against the wooden door. An angry man shouted, "Open up, old woman."
"Evi...go...go hide!"

My grandmother whispered in a sharp tone. I quickly ran and hid in the false cellar. That was the cold, concrete place that I grew to hate. I lived in fear that I was going to be captured by the Communists. They wanted young men and women. I hated that feeling...the terror of being discovered in the false cellar and then taken to a future that I didn't want. I talked myself into being strong and into believing that God had a place for us, too.

******

It has been so good watching you enjoy that bottle of wine tonight. I've missed you. I've missed you these past fifteen years. But now you have come back to me. And the sex has been good. It was always good with you. There, just rest now. You look so comfortable on that sofa. Close your eyes. Rest and relax.

I wanted to tell you the story, my story, about the Civil War. I was just a child but I can't forget what I saw and what I heard. I don't know why I didn't tell you about that when we were together. Oh, I guess I know why. I was too much in love with you. I was too involved with making love to you. I didn't want to talk about the things that haunted me. I didn't want to bring poison from my past into my life with you. I was so afraid of losing you. And, the funny thing

144

is, I did lose you. You took off with your someone else right after the armed robbery. You remember that don't you? The armed robbery? I am sure that I told you about it after it happened. I must have told you about it.

I did lose you, once. I never understood your interest in her. She didn't seem your type. But, now, everything is as it should be. You are through with her, you have reclaimed your feelings for me, and you are here with me tonight. And that it is all that matters to me right now. The stories, the company, the wine-that is all that matters now.

******

"Open up old woman!"
"What do you want?" She shouted through the wooden door.
"Who have you got in there? Open up!"
When she was certain that I was safely hidden, she opened the door slightly. I couldn't see him. I only heard his hostility and anger.
He pushed past her and made his way through the salon and kitchen.
"Who else is here?"
"Nobody...my sons are out with the sheep.
"Give me the bread."

******

"Ladies this is a hold up!
That is what the robbers said to me when they came into the store that I was working at. You remember it don't you? You know the drug store that I worked at. You visited me there on occasion. They were able to identify me as a key holder. I always wondered about that. I had never seen those men before so I often wondered how they were able to identify me and how did they know the lay out of the store so well. Weird isn't it?

Did I ever tell you that he held the knife to my throat? The man with stocking pulled over his head held a knife to my throat. I reached for the telephone to call the police. He slashed the telephone cord. I screamed. He used the weapon to let me know that he wasn't fooling around.

"Give my the Dilaudid and T3s. And, make it fast!"

That scream wrecked my vocal cords. I have a voice disorder now.

******

Earlier that afternoon, my grandmother had carefully placed the ten loaves of bread on the stone kitchen table. Her work began at five o'clock every morning for this was her ritual. She kneaded the dough with her disfigured, arthritic hands, shaped it, and made the sign of the cross on each loaf of bread before she placed them in the stone oven. She did this every morning, without fail. Even when we were a displaced family living in a refugee camp, she got herself up every morning and faced the hopeless dawn to bake ten loaves of bread.

That past year had been a cruel one. My father and uncle both disappeared. We hoped that they are alive somewhere, fighting for some cause. In my heart, I found it hard to hold on to the belief that they were fighting for something because neither of them were political men, just simple shepherds. My grandmother carried them in her spirit and prayed for their safe return every day while she baked the ten loaves of bread.

She was my only adult family since my father disappeared. My mother died of starvation during the famine of 1941. I remember her faintly, just pictures in my mind's eye of a sad, beautiful woman distracted by her inability to feed her three children. I still can see her crying silent tears and trying to comfort our hunger pains with her kisses. But that was a long time ago. My grandmother sustained me with her hope and belief that God had a place for us, too.

******

It was just before the armed robbery. I think it was a week before the armed robbery when you decided to end it between us. That was the time line wasn't it? Yet it had been two weeks prior to that when you called me and told me that you were in love with me. You wanted a future with me. After our three year I don't know what, I thought that maybe I should commit to you. I was going to tell you that I was ready for a commitment but I didn't have a chance to do that. No, of course not. I didn't get my hello into the conversation when you decided that our relationship was not healthy. When had you become the shrink, anyway? You didn't have an exactly healthy track record.

Wasn't it you who was hanging around outside my apartment waiting for the secure doors to open so that you could gain access. I could feel your presence. I just knew that you were near. You later confirmed that for me. You yourself said how strange it was that you were hanging around outside my apartment. Why had you done that? Why didn't you just phone? But, you know, I am really glad that you didn't gain entry because I was saying good-by to the other guy that I was sleeping with. Oh. Are you surprised? Did you really believe that you were the only one?
Two can play the game of deception.
I never trusted you. Call it gut instinct, intuition, or whatever. I never trusted you. From the moment that I met you I had an uneasy feeling about you. I always had a strange insight where you were concerned. I saw you before I met you. I was meditating the night before I first met you. It was your face that I saw. I now know that it was a warning. I hadn't read it that way at the time. But to tell the honest truth, you had a strange hold over me. Your hold on me almost destroyed me. Almost.

******

"Here, take a couple of loaves," she attempted a
negotiation. "I need the rest to feed my sons and the dogs."
"No, I am taking it all." He sounded angrier, even
more aggressive.
"Please, take what you need for today. I have to
feed my sons and dogs."
He pushed her against the wall and knocked her to
the floor. I heard a painful moan as she fell. She hurt her
head, hurt it on the stone table.
"You greedy son-of-a-bitch...You won't live long
enough to finish the first loaf."
"That's what you think, old bitch. I'll be back
tomorrow. Have ten more loaves ready for me."
She tried to get up. He kicked her in the stomach.
He spit on her. He slammed the door.
"My God is bigger than you are!" She shouted,
defiantly.

******

This time around, before you showed up again, I
knew that you were lurking. I never saw you but I knew that
you were driving up and down my street. I knew that you
were going to seek me out a month before you actually
turned up. Call it second sight, destiny, or whatever you
want. Even when you chose to end it before the robbery, I
knew that it wasn't over between us. I knew then, that I had
unfinished business with you. Just like my grandmother had
unfinished business with the bastard you beat her and stole
the ten loaves of bread.

Ok. So, I have been sleeping with you, showering
with you, eating with you since this past fall. You have
shared your regrets with me and you think that we have
rekindled what we lost all those years ago.

So why did you feel it necessary to come back to me
after you left me for her? I never understood why you left me
in the first place. She looked like the mother earth statues
that I've seen at the museum. You know the ones I am
talking about. Huge breasts. Sagging stomach. There was

something very primitive looking about her. I wondered if you were looking for a mother.

I wasn't a mother figure to you. Anything but that. No. I was your sex toy. I stripped for you. I had casual sex with you. You really didn't want a relationship with me. You were looking for sex. Or were you?

Since your return, I thought about how so many things about you just didn't add up. I was thin. You went on and on about that. Yet, you left me for someone like her. You didn't want a relationship with me back then, so I started thinking. Why do you want one with me now?

Are you feeling a little uncomfortable? Have I hit a little too close to the truth? Maybe I wasn't such a dumb fuck after all.

I suspected that you were up to no good from the beginning. Back then and especially this time around. But I needed to be certain of what you had done to me.
You know, the cops that did the investigation said that the two robbers never told them who they were fencing for.

You were behind that robbery weren't you? You set the whole thing up. You never left me for her. You were always with her.

You arranged to damage me mentally, psychologically, financially. You almost destroyed me. But you didn't.

You see, now the tables are turned.

******

I counted slowly. My body chilled against the cold pavement. Safe time. I had to wait for enough safe time to pass.

"Yiayia," I spoke softly. I wanted to reach out to her. To comfort her in some way.

She sat in the chair next to the salon window and watched the angry, young man make his way through the fields behind our house. She wasn't crying. Famine, loss,

149

and the Civil War had dried up her tears. Only a numbed faith remained. We watched him make himself comfortable under the shade of the orange tree at the end of the field.

"Yiayia, how can he even swallow that bread knowing what he did to you?"

'People kill for a piece of bread. I offered him food. He could have left enough for us, too."

******

Do you know what happened to the man that beat my grandmother? He was bombed. Blown away. Right in front of us. I saw it happen.

My grandmother was very fortunate to see such swift retribution. She was old and didn't have years to see payback. She cursed him and her curse took. You know, I read somewhere that once a curse is given it can never be reversed. The same holds true for a blessing.

I have been cursing you for years. But when none of my curses stuck, I took matters into my own hands.

That wine that you nursed tonight was laced with a lethal dose of Phenobarbital. A ten fold lethal dose. You know that drug, don't you? Your friends asked me for that drug too when they held the knife to my throat and the gun to my head.

So, you see, I have had good reason to end things with you once and for all.

Sleep well.

Shared Values
by Nicole Chardenet

I moved to Canada from the States and settled in Mississauga in the spring of 2005. When people ask me why, I either give them the short smartass answer ("Better beer") or I give them the longer answer ("Mid-life crisis, better professional opportunities, and I'm really diggin' this democracy thing you've got going on").

Crossing the border went smoothly, if you don't mind moving from central Connecticut to southern Ontario in the truck of a certain do-it-yourself moving company with a bad reputation regarding lousy customer service, customer abuse and, even more frightening, death trap moving trucks, all of which I discovered only days before leaving. The truck turned out to be the *only* aspect of this moving company that wasn't singularly unpleasant. I won't even mention the nasty-tempered drooling (literally) backwoods freak in the rural wilds of Connecticut from whom I had to pick up the truck.

I was gratified, a month after my arrival, to read in the paper that the Ministry of Transportation threatened to prohibit this company's trucks from operating in Ontario unless the company addressed certain safety violations.

Nevertheless, I got to the border okay and the unsmiling Immigration Man <cue Crosby, Stills, Nash & Young please> in Buffalo was not at all impressed to be faced with yet another American immigrant. (There goes the country!) However, he cracked the smallest semblance of a smile when I redeemed myself slightly by sporting a desperately French name.

"Got your list of personal possessions?" he asked me, and I produced my excruciatingly organized accordion folder of personal papers, clearly marked and tabbed for easy identification.

I pulled out my painfully constructed list of boxes and bundles, each marked with a number (with a corresponding hastily-inscribed number on each box in the van) and describing, in almost anal-retentive detail, the contents of each, lest they should think I'm actually an Al-Qaeda terrorist who's *really* bringing C-4 and capsules of live avian flu virus (anthrax is *sooooo* 2003!) into the country rather than "Dish towels & kitchen utensils" in Box #58.

I held my breath while he scanned the list. The truth was, I *did* have one possession I was afraid might raise an eyebrow – a rusty decorative scimitar which I used as a prop for belly dancing in my younger days. I don't think you could actually kill anyone with it, unless they hadn't had a tetanus shot lately. I debated leaving it back in Connecticut but I kept promising myself I'd get back into belly dancing eventually, and some day I *would* re-learn how to dance with a scimitar on my head and other various jiggling body parts without danger of damaging the furniture or slicing the cat in half.

I'd instructed the young boys I'd hired to load the moving van for me to put the scimitar at the back of the truck, so that if Immigration or Customs wanted to see it, it would be easily accessible, and I could let them keep it if they really were desperately afraid I was going to try to infect the Canadian population with a nasty case of lockjaw.

Instead, he commented, "This is the most legible and organized list of personal possessions I've ever seen!"

"Thank you," I replied, relieved he wasn't going to ask me about my Weapon of Largely Localised Destruction. "Um, wanna see the Rabies Certificate for my cat?"

"No, that won't be necessary," he told me, which I thought was unusual, since it was specifically required of me to cross over, and I realized that the Canadian border really *was* as porous as certain critics in the Bush administration claimed, considering how easy it was cross with rusty tetanus-laden scimitars and potentially rabid felines.

Customs was as much of a snap as Immigration was, and I was rubber-stamped all over the place and allowed to venture forth into my new Canadian home – and promptly almost got blown into Lake Ontario by high winds as I crossed the Garden City Skyway. Welcome to Canada, Nicole.

A year later, I love my adopted country and freely appreciate the freedoms one still has here that one no longer has in the U.S., like the right to check out a library book without the feds descending on your neighbourhood demanding to know why a Real American would want to read a terrorist-loving freedom-hating piece of trash like *Bush's Brain* or anything by Al Franken.

Or being able to listen to Air America without having to worry about the CIA showing up in the middle of the night, throwing you onto a rendition flight bound for Syria or Afghanistan, and 'interrogating' you with state-of-the-art investigation techniques that don't run afoul of 'quaint' basic human decency standards like those of the Geneva Convention.

Although I admit sometimes I wonder why some people move here in the first place if they don't favour Canadian values. Like last year, when some argued that we need to allow sharia law which somehow won't conflict with Canadian values despite this particular religious law having about as much in common with the Charter of Rights & Freedoms as *Mein Kampf*.

As an example of the sort of person who picked the wrong damn country to immigrate to, last fall I was on the bus and sitting across from me was a tired-looking man who moved to a seat near

me, probably for more room. About ten minutes before I got to my stop in Mississauga, he looked at the pentagram ring I was wearing and asked if it was the symbol of the Antichrist.

"The WHAT?" I asked, stunned.

"Your star. What is it?"

"That's a pentagram."

"Do you believe in that stuff?"

What stuff? Magic? Right-wing politics? Stephen Harper's belief that there's not enough evidence to support global warming? I said, "I'm a Pagan."

"A what?"

"I'm a Pagan." Or more to the point, a Wiccan, Wicca being a modern religion based on ancient European pagan beliefs and practices, and ignoring the icky (and now illegal) parts like human sacrifice and institutionalised gender discrimination.

He looked slightly alarmed. "Do you believe in God?"

"I believe in the Mother Goddess and the Father God."

"WHAT?"

"I believe God is both male and female."

So he immediately launched into this weird rant about how God is not one thing or another. Fair enough, I thought, although he's not letting me get a word in edgewise to explain that ultimately I *don't* think the Deity has a sex, but I can also see--a brightly-coloured striped hat and I hear a Jamaican accent and what I thought was fatigue on his face before I am beginning to think is the effects of de holy ganja. At least *one* of us is acting like we're on drugs, and I'm entirely certain it's not *me*.

No biggie. Better ganja than demon rum, right?

He asked, switching topics on me suddenly, "Do you believe in gay rights?"

"Yes," I told him. "Everyone should have equal rights."

This launched another tirade about how God destroyed an entire city because of homosexuality.

"You're a Christian, aren't you," I smile, unruffled. What a sight this must be to all the Hindus & Muslims sitting around us. I'm pretty sure it's illegal, under penalty of being beaten to death by Wayne Gretzky with a hockey stick, to discuss religion in any way, shape or form in a public place in Canada unless you are waxing righteously about Peter McGuinty's plan that did away with religious arbitration.

"No, I'm not a Christian," he answered. "I just read Scripture."

"I've read it too. So what's your point? It's not your holy book, or mine - I don't have to believe in it."

"There is none of that man with man stuff in the Old Testament! Don't you realize God destroyed that city for this?"

"There is no evidence of that."

"What do you mean? I've *been* there!"

"You've *seen* the remains of Sodom and Gomorrah? Hon, they don't *exist*. There is *no* archaeological record of their existence." I don't tell him I got that word directly from an Orthodox Jew years ago who dearly wanted everything in the Old Testament to be historically true. Louis was in that part of the Sinai desert as well and if *he* couldn't find the archaeological remnants of S&G, believe me, baby, they ain't there.

Another rant. I didn't catch all of what he said but he still tried to justify his views with Bible
passages to a declared non-believer. His voice got loud and agitated. I wasn't worried he was going to get violent, but I've never had anyone get this crazy on me before if they weren't a flaming Bible-thumper. Not even from American Southerners. There they tend to bite their tongues and get sweeter and sweeter the madder they're getting at you, until they're so sticky-sweet you know if you open your mouth any further they're going to jam a platter of fried chicken down your throat.

Then he launched into this business about how the U.S. is going to suffer for its sins.

"You're probably right," I tell him, thinking, post-Katrina, that Louisiana was already learning the wages of the sin of voting for George Bush. Or Florida getting whacked by five hurricanes the year after the last election, where the state voted for Bush. Sort of.

"And Toronto's going to get it too. For legalizing gay marriage."

"God hasn't struck us down yet."

"You wait! He's going to! The prophecies are all there in the Bible!"

I didn't ask him to point out where in the Bible it's predicted that Toronto is going to get Sodomized.

I also didn't ask him if he believes the Bible passage that says all black people should be enslaved because of their lineage tracing back to Ham and his sin of uncovering his father's nakedness. Hey, we *all* pick and choose what we believe from the Bible.

Fortunately, my stop was next. I rang the bell.

"Read the Bible! It's all in the prophecies!" he tells me.

"Jesus said 2,000 years ago he's coming back before the end of the next generation, and we're still waiting," I smiled as I stood up. "You have a nice day."

Some people should have just stayed home.

The Struggle Within

by Irv Haberman

"Hey! Where do you think you're going?" The burly factory worker walked over and stood defiantly in front of my wheelchair, blocking my way.

"The leader sent for me," I replied. The al-Qaeda leader was never referred to by name.

The worker immediately stepped aside, muttered an apology and joined the others, busy in kneading and weaving together the pastry, then sliding it into brick ovens. They were making baqlawa, the Iraqi version of baklava.

I proceeded to a back room in this central Baghdad factory and knocked on the door.

"Come!" a deep voice commanded.

Unsure as to why I was summoned, I hesitantly opened the door and entered.

The al-Qaeda leader, a stout man, sat alone at a table eating the sweet pastry. He motioned for me to pull my wheelchair across from him.

Before words could be spoken, there was another knock on the door. A messenger entered and reported on the young man, who had just walked into a crowded restaurant and detonated his suicide vest. "The nails, screws and bolts, together with the sticks of explosives, maximized the slaughter," the messenger stated matter-of-factly. "The explosion flung body parts into Abu Nuwas Street."

The stout man slid his chair back from the table, tilted his head back and gave off a bellowing laugh. He was unconcerned that the gooey concoction of pistachio nuts, honey and pastry dough was running down the corners of his mouth, into his full beard.

After dismissing the messenger with a wave of his hand, he turned to me. "I have received a message from our glorious leader. He asked for divine punishment against those who collaborate with the United States. And," he said, pointing his finger for emphasis, "he announced a step-up in our method of attacks."

156

I sat in my wheelchair, listening obediently.

"After many months", he continued, his eyes wide with excitement, "a new and spectacular method of attack against the West has finally been perfected. I have sent for you because I share your pain over the brutal slaughter of your wife and daughter by those western aggressors." He stroked his beard, then announced: "I have selected you, Daoud Jaradat, to carry out my plan and achieve martyrdom."

I could feel tears beginning to swell in my eyes. It was only two weeks ago that I had come home to find my beloved wife and five-year-old daughter on the floor, their bodies riddled with bullets. My heart was shattered. My grief was devastating. The al-Qaeda leader had told me that they were murdered by soldiers from the West. Now, I was being offered a way to retaliate against those barbarians. "I am honoured. But, why me?" I asked, puzzled. "I'm thirty-six-years-old and since childhood, I've endured the disease of polio. The resulting paralysis and muscular atrophy has confined me to this bloody contraption." I banged my fist against the arm of the wheelchair.

"I'll tell you why I've chosen you," replied the al-Qaeda leader as he looked deep into my eyes. "Your confinement to the wheelchair is instrumental to the success of my plan. I am confident that you can be trusted. As well, you are educated with college experience, coming from a middle class background. You speak a Londoner's English, with only a trace of Arabic. Lastly, your demeanour is impressive; you can handle yourself in a confident manner and are at ease around people. That, Jaradat, is why you were chosen."

I was honoured by the confidence he was showing in me. As I awaited the details of this spectacular plan, I felt a surge of emotion to wreak revenge on the western aggressors and to join my family in Heaven.

The stout man leaned forward in his chair and spoke softly. "Allah has promised either Paradise or Hell to his creatures. I am offering you the way to open the door to Paradise, the shortest path to Heaven."

I nodded.

The al-Qaeda leader began to explain his plan.

As I was listening to the details, I squirmed slightly in my wheelchair and hoped the involuntary reaction wasn't noticed. I felt beads of perspiration beginning to form on my forehead and resisted the urge to wipe them away. This plan of his was shocking, horrifying. It was not at all what I had expected. Be very careful, I must not show my displeasure.

His explanation now finished, he sat back in his chair.

I was unable to speak. I found myself torn between his wishes and my beliefs. It was true that life here was just a pathway to life in the next world, the true life. And, as most did, I endorsed the common fight for sovereignty. I also wanted revenge against those brutal aggressors. But I also believed in the strict interpretation of the holy Koran, that taught it was unlawful to kill innocent people. What was I to do? I dare not refuse the al-Qaeda leader. He had a reputation for brutality and was feared. My head began to throb.

"When I close my eyes," the stout man announced, both hands raised to Heaven, "all I will see will be the faces of the thousand innocents who, in God's name, will be killed. Daoud Jaradat will become a glorious martyr."

The nine hundred and sixty foot cruise ship was docked in Antigua, one of its five ports of call. Many of the twenty-three hundred passengers had already disembarked, eager to explore the island or relax on one of the more than three hundred white sand beaches.

I was enjoying a leisurely breakfast in the dining room when I recalled my reaction upon first boarding the ship two days earlier. My mouth had dropped open in amazement for I had never seen such opulence before. As I toured the ship during that first day, I had found it fascinating to watch people partake in the self indulgence and shameless pampering. I finished my breakfast with another gourmet scone and washed it down with cappuccino. As I wiped my mouth with the linen napkin, I couldn't help but smile. I shamefully concluded that this was easy to get used to.

My smile suddenly faded as I was brought back to reality. It would all be over tonight.

I glanced at my watch and realized that I must be off to my appointment. The glass elevator took me to level two, where I went down the ramp and departed the ship.

Standing between the end of the pier and the streets of town was Heritage Quay, a compilation of small shops designed to separate the cruise passengers from their money. I felt like a kid with a new toy as I skirted around the strolling tourists and made my way to the street. The al-Qaeda leader had given this motorized scooter to me before I began my journey. It was much lighter and easier to use than the wheelchair that I had been a prisoner to for so many years.

Once I reached the street, I turned right and went down a block. The old, two-storey building appeared deserted. I followed a narrow pathway, hidden by weeds, that ran along the side of the structure and knocked on the side door.

"Who's there?" It was a young male voice.

"It's Daoud Jaradat. I was sent here." I could picture an eye examining me through the newly installed peep hole in the door.

The door was swung open by an Antiguan in his late-twenties. He promptly set down a wooden ramp over the step, allowing me to enter on the scooter.

An old wooden chair was the only piece of furniture in the room. A single light bulb dangled from the ceiling. My attention became riveted on a motorized scooter in the middle of the room. It looked identical to the one I was sitting on.

The Antiguan saw my reaction and walked over to the new scooter. "Looks exactly like yours, right?" Not waiting for a reply, he continued. "And, just like yours, this battery pack is exactly the same size." He bent down and ran his hand lightly over the nearly thirteen-inch-long battery pack that was snapped into place on the front of the scooter. "There is one important difference: only the top third of this battery pack is the actual battery. The bottom two-thirds is filled with plastic explosives."

He stood up. "You are familiar with how C-4 operates and how to detonate it?"

"Yes." Everything had been explained to me, repeatedly, by the al-Qaeda leader. I continued to stare at the new scooter. I could see no difference at all between it and the one I was sitting on.

"It's very important to remember that, with only a third of the battery pack being the actual battery, you must recharge it more often."

"Yes, I'll remember."

"When you board the ship riding your new scooter, you should pass through security without a problem," the young man added.

"I don't anticipate a problem. When I first boarded the ship in San Juan, they checked my scooter with a hand-held detector. Since then, they just let me pass without any check at all."

The Antiguan brought the new scooter closer and helped me onto it. He then handed me a shopping bag. "Just to be safe, take this bag. There's a short-sleeved shirt in it, your size, purchased from a men's store in Heritage Quay. It would be only natural that you bought something while off the ship. When you board, their attention will be on the bag, not on the scooter. Okay then, you're set."

I was ready, but my stomach began to ache with the knowledge of what was to follow that evening.

"Allah be with you," the young man said, opening the door and watching me leave on the new scooter. He promptly brought in the wooden ramp and locked the door. A van would arrive soon to take away both the ramp and the old scooter. Then his part of the plan would be completed.

I was in my cabin that evening, getting ready for the formal dinner. It was during this dinner – after the serving of the main course – that I was to excuse myself for not feeling well, get back onto the scooter and detonate the C-4, high velocity plastic explosives. The bi-level dining room would be full of well-dressed, unsuspecting passengers. I shuddered in the thought of what the result would be. I recalled the al-Qaeda leader telling me proudly that it was C-4 that was used in the October 2000 bombing of the battleship USS Cole.

My hands were shaking as I finally managed to attach my bow tie. Ever since I had left the meeting with the al-Qaeda leader, I had been successful in putting the inner conflict with my beliefs aside. Instead, I had concentrated on the joy of joining my wife and child in Heaven. Now, as the moment was near, I began to find it impossible to dismiss my beliefs. My thoughts centered on a principle in the holy Koran: *regardless of how legitimate the cause may be, the killing of innocent people is never condoned.* Here I was, moments away from wreaking death and destruction on a thousand innocents.

I shrugged in an attempt to brush the thoughts aside. Fully dressed, I sprayed perfume on my newly shaved head and formal clothing. The smell of flower water was the pre-martyrdom ritual, ablution, that prepared me for Paradise. Then, taking a deep breath, I left the cabin on my scooter to go to the dining room.

What have I gotten myself into? I was no rebel, no hero. I was just a weak man with a disability. But, always a devout man, conscious of doing right. Can I consider what I was about to do as being 'right'? My head was spinning as I entered the dining room and made my way to my table.

As he had done each evening before, the retired insurance executive, who sat beside me at the dining room table, got up and held my chair while I managed to slide off the scooter onto it. This time, the "thank you" I uttered was less enthusiastic, knowing that my instructions were to excuse myself just before finishing the main course, get back onto my scooter and... No! I must not think about it!

When the shrimp cocktail appetizer was served, I dipped a shrimp into the cocktail sauce, took a bite, but tasted nothing. Purposely, I tried to avoid eye contact with the others at my table. The man from New York, sitting across from me, told a joke and the others laughed. I could not bear the merriment – not so close to the time of bloodshed.

My eyes happened to wander to people sitting at a table to my right. My gaze locked on a young girl, likely five years old, who sat facing me. I hadn't noticed her before; she must have sat at a different seat at the table. It was a pink bow, sitting prominently in her brown hair, that grabbed my attention. A flood of memories returned. My treasure, my five-year-old daughter, was very fond of a pink bow. She had always asked that it be placed in her brown hair.

While I was staring, the mother leaned over and lovingly gave the young girl a kiss on the cheek. At that instant, I froze. The appetizer fork dropped out of my hand, landing noiselessly on the tablecloth.

The young girl saw me. She smiled.

My stomach sank. An innocent child. How could I murder her ... and her mother. Would I not be as guilty as those brutal aggressors who had killed my daughter and wife? I closed my eyes, hoping this inner conflict would end. My mind would only focus on the teachings of the Prophet: *even in a state of war, one shall not kill any old person, any woman or any child.*

My insides felt queasy. I used my napkin to dry my eyes from the sweat that was running into them. I can't stand this turmoil any longer. I must leave the table. I will excuse myself now, saying that I am not feeling well.

Wait! It is too early; the main course has not yet been served. I must follow the al-Qaeda leader's instructions precisely.

No matter. I must leave the table **now!**

The cool breeze felt refreshing against my face. I must have taken the glass elevator to the top level of the ship and then out onto the deserted deck. The turbulence in my mind would not let me remember. As I came to the middle of the ship, instinctively, I moved toward the railing.

In the moonlight, I gazed down at the ocean below. It looked so peaceful. As I stared at the water, I could feel the stupor gradually easing, my mind clearing. My eyes filled with tears; the inner calm was so welcomed. Finally, the struggle within had ceased.

I now realized what my course of action must be. At that instant, I closed my wet eyes and felt complete contentment envelop me. I wanted to remain that way, but my mind snapped to attention. It was time for action.

First, I turned the key to shut off the power to the scooter, locking the wheels. Then, holding onto the railing of the ship, I lifted myself off the scooter.

As I leaned back against the railing for support, I unsnapped the battery pack. Using both hands, I lifted it from the front of the scooter. My grip was not as strong as it once was and I felt the battery pack starting to slip from my hands. If it fell to the floor, I would not be able to lift it.

I gritted my teeth and, mustering all my strength, I managed to get it over the railing. I ignored the searing pain in my arms and shoulders. Instead, I uttered a deep sigh of relief as the battery pack, with the explosives inside, splashed into the ocean and sank below the surface of the water.

It would no longer be used to kill innocent people.

I got back onto the immobile scooter to rest. Just then, a voice yelled out. "Hey, what's going on?"

A ship officer, his arm waving, was walking hurriedly along the deck toward me.

Quickly, I reached into the pocket of my tuxedo coat, fumbling for a small object. I felt a strange comfort as my fingers clutched it and removed it from the pocket. The al-Qaeda leader had instructed that it be used only in the unlikely event that the detonator was faulty.

Wasting no time, I peeled back the protective covering and put the small white pill on my tongue.

I then began to whisper prayers.

The ship officer approached me. "Are you all right? Did something fall overboard?"

I ignored the questions. Instead, I closed my eyes and continued with my prayers. The pill would be dissolved soon.

I derived strength from knowing that I had followed the teachings of the holy Koran and, as a result, would enter Paradise and, ultimately, Heaven.

My heart was singing. I would soon be holding my beloved wife and daughter in my arms again.

Time to Say Goodbye . . .

by Rosanna Battigelli

His eyes are partially closed when I arrive. I approach the bed, wondering if I should just leave him be; perhaps he needs to sleep, perhaps he didn't sleep much during the night . . . He starts as the shadow thrown by my body snuffs out the light entering the slit in his eyes. His eyelids flutter, a muffled greeting forms in his throat but never leaves his mouth.

His left hand lifts ever so slightly. It is an artist's palette, splattered with bruises of magenta and vermilion-tinged brown, puddles of eggplant purple and yellow-green; his fingers, swollen and pale, resemble a giant paw; his wrist, dotted with the puncture marks from previous intravenous needles, is a freeway of veins. There is an IV attached now, carrying precious potassium to his deprived body.

His muffled warbling continues, and his eyes begin to open. I lean forward, trying to ascertain their clarity, almost as if I expect the nebulous depths to dissipate just for me, so I can find the treasures that I know exist there. Open, Sesame! Come on, a little more, that's it. His eyelashes rise and fall and then hold steady. I peer closely and only see the treasures that cataracts and glaucoma bring–murky opal stones with no fire.

Hey, Dad, how are you doing?

I bend to kiss him on the cheek, and he moves his head slightly, a short jerk. I take it as a sign of recognition; he may not know who I am, but my voice is familiar.

It's me, Dad. I came to spend some time with you . . . Here, let me take your hand; it's so dry, just like mine. Why don't I put some cream on it? This hospital cream isn't bad; I'll just massage it on your skin. There, isn't that better? Now let me do your other hand . . .

Hey, Dad, I saw a rabbit yesterday in my yard . . . It's so nice, living out in the country; you get to see all kinds of wild animals. Let's see, what have we spotted in the forest . . . bears, two deer, a moose and her calf, a fox . . . Do you remember when you used to go hunting in the old country, Dad? With your dog Argo?

Is that a flicker of a nod my Dad makes? Is he understanding my monologue? I have become used to half-hour soliloquies; he cannot respond, with a nasal gastric tube that has been inserted in his nose and down his throat to carry liquid food to his stomach.

Maybe I shouldn't be talking about food, when he lacks the power to control the mechanisms involved in one of the greatest of all pleasures, eating.

His swallowing processes no longer function; eating out of a spoon puts him at a high risk for aspirating, the speech pathologist has determined after performing a swallowing assessment. The cause? Most likely a combination of factors, she explains kindly: the advanced stage of his Parkinson's disease; the heart attack he suffered two years earlier; the small stroke that went undetected . . .

I'm afraid we'll eventually lose the battle, Dad's doctor has informed us at a family conference. His body is quitting on him. Your Dad doesn't want a tube in his nose; he has pulled it out, which is why we have no choice but to restrain his arms. We're keeping him alive by mechanical means, but even what he is getting will not be able to sustain him forever . . . his condition is palliative . . .

I look at those cloth restraints now, holding my Dad's wrists securely by his side, strapped around the metal frame of the bed.

Hey, Dad, your hands are cool; let me pull up this blanket. It's getting cooler outside; Mom wants me to pluck the rest of the tomatoes off the vines so they don't freeze tonight. Imagine, Dad, it's only the beginning of September, and the forecast says it could go down to four below zero. You know Mom, eh Dad, how she curses Christopher Columbus every time it gets too cold, because if he hadn't discovered America, we would have never left Italy, where it never freezes in September.

I wish I could remember the voyage. I know I was only three, and Mom tells me the name of the ship was Saturnia . . . and that I was the only one in our family who didn't get seasick. I love the sea; if I could, I'd go back there every summer . . .

It's funny to think of all the silly things that caused us angst growing up, eh Dad? Do you remember in 1970 when bell-bottom pants were in style?

I begged Mom to get me some, or even make them for me, so I could be like the rest of the kids in my Grade Five class, and she told me I'd have to ask you when you got home from work. I spent a couple of hours worrying about whether you would consent or not . . . and you did!

I know you wanted to make your children happy, Dad, and when you and Mom were starting to get on your feet, and you had bought your first house in 1969 for $22,000.00, we felt like we were rich. Not arrogant rich, but the feeling of being rich enough to have our own house instead of renting. I think we could sense your pride, Dad, to have been able to find a house with an apartment on the top floor you could rent out to help with the mortgage, and a back yard big enough to make a decent garden, and a detached garage–a shack, really–but it served its purpose, even housing chickens and rabbits for a while . . .

And you and Mom finally had your own room to yourselves. I shared a brightly-painted pink room with Pina, and the two boys shared–what else?–a blue room. I'll never forget the colour of the living room and kitchen when we bought the house–lime green and purple, respectively. Well, it was 1969 after all; psychedelic colours were popular back then.

Mom wanted the house freshly painted, remember, all neutral colours except for the pink and blue bedrooms. We had a lot of happy times in that house, eh Dad? The birthdays, the Christmas and the Easter celebrations, the Confirmations, the weddings, the wine-making . . .

Sad times, too, though . . .

You lost your eldest daughter Pina while we were still at that house, and I my sister. The spring of 1975. I'll never forget that dismal, rainy April day, coming home from high school and hearing the news. Even now that I'm a parent, I can only imagine the pain you and Mom must have felt, losing a child on the brink of young adulthood . . . from blood poisoning caused by a ruptured appendix . . . in this day and age . . .

You know, Dad, we never talked about it before; after all, I was only fifteen at the time, and she was seventeen . . . but I remember how dark life was for a while, no smiles for many months, no laughter, no parties, no television . . . But eventually the smiles returned; I remember cheering inwardly for the return of your spirit, yours and Mom's, and the discarding of the black mourning clothes . . . although I realize that mourning for a loved one may subside, but it doesn't ever really go away . . .

I was relieved that you and Mom could find some measure of happiness again, and I can't tell you the joy I felt a decade later, watching you with your first grandchild, my Sarah.

Hey, Dad, you're tired; your eyes are closing. I'm going to let you have a rest now. I'll come back soon and we'll spend some more time together. Next time I'll bring my portable disc player, so you can hear some nice Italian music. How about some Andrea Bocelli? What a beautiful voice he has . . .

Good night Dad; let me give you a kiss. I love you, you hear? *Ti voglio tanto bene.*

Will my father make it through the night? As I gaze with misty eyes on his curved, still figure, the words of one of my favourite Andrea Bocelli songs resound in my head:

Time to say goodbye . . .
I'll go with you on ships across seas which . . . exist no longer;
with you I shall experience them again.
I'll go with you, I with you.*

As I leave my father, my eyes spill salty tears from a sea of memories.

Arrivederci, Papà.

The End

*from the song "TIME TO SAY GOODBYE (CON TE PARTIRO')"
(Sartori - Quarantotto - Peterson)
(c) Sugar s.r.l. - Double Marpot s.r.l.
Used by permission

Contributors

Fay Manawwar

Fay Manawwar is a retired family physician, who once published her poems in college magazines.

Enid Chan

Enid Chan is a retired obstetrician and gynecologist.

Bianca Lakoseljac

Bianca Lakoseljac is a Masters of Arts graduate and the recipient of the Matthew Ahern Memorial Award in Literature from York University. She has taught a variety of writing courses at Humber College and Ryerson University. Bianca is currently completing her first novel, *The Dancing Bear*, which chronicles the "rite of passage" of a fourteen-year old girl befriended by a Gypsy clan. She is also working on a collection of interconnected short stories.

Flavia Cosma

Flavia Cosma (www.flaviacosma.com) is a Romanian born Canadian poet. She obtained her Masters in electrical engineering at the Polytechnic Institute of Bucharest. She studied drama for two years. She is an independent producer/director/writer of TV documentaries. To date, she has published nine books of poetry, a novel, a travel memoir and a book of Fairy Tales. Her poetry book" 47 POEMS" (Texas Tech University Press), won the prestigious ALTA Richard Wilbur Poetry in Translation Prize.

Liisa Hypponen

Liisa Hypponen, a native of Toronto, began her life-long dream of writing in May 2004, by taking a magazine article writing course at Ryerson University. Liisa's work has appeared in Reader's Digest, Life's Like That, and The Toronto Star's Your Home section. Liisa works at a provincial teachers' association, but continues to hone her writing skills at Ryerson and through her involvement in the Canadian Authors Association.

Margo Georgakis

Margo has completed a collection of short stories and is currently working on a novel. In the last two years, she has had a number of short stories, as well poetry, accepted for publication in Europe (in English as well as Greek translation).

Nancy L. Hull

A long-time member of Canadian Authors Association, Nancy L. Hull is a published author, artist, photographer, involved with environmental issues, wildlife, equine, and animal welfare concerns. She holds two degrees from York University Toronto, as well as additional qualifications in many disciplines. Originally a Torontonian, she currently lives on Georgian Bay, Ontario.

Pat Hart

Pat Hart was born and raised in Alberta. She graduated from the Alberta College of Art, then married, and had a family. Later, she joined the faculty of "The School of Design and Fine Arts" at Georgian College, Barrie, Ontario where she taught for twenty-three years. After retirement, Pat took a series of creative writing courses and suddenly she was hooked on the art of writing.

Jake Hogeterp

Finding a continuing ed. catalogue ten years ago that included a short story course gave me the final impetus to get writing. Today I peck at my keyboard daily, share my efforts with The Scarborough Writers Association weekly and live the joys and frustrations of the part-time writing life constantly, while continuing to meet mundane needs through employment in the food industry. I'm new to CAA this year, hoping thus to reach that next plateau.

Ben Antao

Ben Antao is a veteran journalist and writer of both fiction and non-fiction. He's the author of *Images of Goa* (1990), a memoir, and *Goa, A Rediscovery* (2004), a travelogue. His debut novel *Blood & Nemesis* (2005) is about Goa's freedom struggle from the Portuguese rule. A second novel *Penance,* about a love triangle that ends in tragedy was published in 2006. He is the current president of the Canadian Authors Association, Toronto Branch.

Shane Joseph

Shane Joseph is a graduate of the Humber School for Writers. He published his first novel "Redemption in Paradise" in 2004. He has completed a second novel and a collection of short stories. His work has appeared in *Existere* magazine and in short story anthologies in Canada and Sri Lanka.

Graham J. Ducker

Retired principal /teacher.Published memoirs 'Don't Wake The Teacher' 2004 (Hidden Brook Press). Avid poet and writer of short stories. International Rhyming Poetry Judge, Federation of Poets, Nov. 2005. Published in international magazines, anthologies and E-zines. Awarded first place in The International Lichen Epistolary Fiction 2006 Contest. Co-Founder / Publisher of The Durham Region Poetry Digest (Printed & Online) A book of his poetry is to be published by end of 2006.

Nicole Chardenet

Nicole Chardenet was born in Florida and moved to Ontario from Connecticut. Her professional life spanned the exciting fields of country-western disc jockey and belly dancing before settling on the glamorous world of computer geekery. She currently resides in Mississauga with a roommate and two feline fur-bearing poopmonsters. She says she really did move here for better beer.

Kathy Buckworth

Kathy Buckworth the author of *The Secret Life of SuperMom* (Sourcebooks, 2005), and *SuperMom: A Celebration of All You Do* (Sourcebooks, 2006). Her third book, *Journey to the Darkside: SuperMom Goes Home* will be published by Key Porter in July, 2007. Kathy won the Professional Writers Association of Canada 2006 Award for Excellence in Humour. Kathy is a regular contributor to many publications and websites, including Today's Parent and canadianliving. She lives and works in Mississauga, Ontario. www.kathybuckworth.com.

John Jansen in de Wal

John grew up in Holland, a multi-lingual teacher. Adventure brought him to Canada where he first did the immigrant thing; working in a host of trades. He retired from teaching to write full time. John has published fiction, poetry and articles. He has edited newsletters and served as reader for a number of writing contests. John and Frieda have four children and eight grandchildren. His hobbies are travel and photography.

Gerry Markee

Gerry Markee lives in Toronto with his wife, children and three cats. He has worked in the security industry, in hospitals, office towers and even a chocolate factory, but they were only jobs. His greatest love and hope is to be able to make his living as a fantasy writer without working for the government.

Gabriella Papic

Gabriella Papic is a writer based in Toronto, Ontario.

M. Baghat

I was born and raised in Egypt. Graduated from Cairo University in 1964 with a BSW. Immigrated to Canada in 1970. Graduated York University in 1978 with a BA, and in 1980 with a BA. Hon. Psychology. Published two articles, Write Faster, & Get Organized, in the Canadian Writers Journal in 2000 & 2001. I work as a Youth Probation Officer for Ontario Government.

Deborah Cannon

Deborah Cannon is a graduate of the Humber School for Writers. Her love of the Pacific landscape and her experience as an archaeologist inspired her first novel The Raven's Pool. Her short stories appear at fictionwise.com and Tales from the Manchester Arms, a Toronto CAA anthology. She is published by SFU Archaeology Press, the Canadian Journal of Archaeology, the Canadian Writer's Guide and Absolutewrite.com. Her most recent novel White Raven has just been released.

Bill MacDonald

Bill has been a Sorbonne student, school teacher, Arctic weatherman, and immigration officer. He presently lives and writes in Thunder Bay. In 2005 he won first prize for short fiction in the Elora Writers' Festival competition. His stories have appeared in GEIST, TEN STORIES HIGH and TALES FROM THE MANCHESTER ARMS. His novel, SOOTHSAYER, was published by Borealis Press last spring. His new novel, BARNABAS SNUG HARBOUR, will be published by Borealis this fall.

M.E. Kowalski

M.E. Kowalski lives with his two children in Toronto, where he founded and continues to manage the Toronto Writers' Centre. A former real estate lawyer, Kowalski has written a number of non-fiction pieces for a variety of legal publications, The Globe and Mail and National Post. He is currently working on his first novel, set in modern day Philippines.

George Bernstein

A retired orthopedic surgeon based in Toronto, his stories, essays, poetry and book reviews have appeared in: The Literary Review of Canada, Parchment, Mediphors, Jewish Frontier (NYC), Journal of Medicine for the Performing Arts, Military Medicine, Expressions, University of Chicago Perspectives, Canadian Medical Association Journal, North West Poetry Review, and others...he has also won a number of writing awards.

Allyson Latta

Born in Edmonton, Alberta, Allyson Latta is a former newspaper and magazine editor and writer who holds degrees in both criminology and journalism. Over the past few years, as a book editor she has worked on best-selling titles including short-listers and winners of the Giller Prize and the Governor General's Literary Awards. She also developed and teaches a course in memoir writing for Ryerson University. Allyson has travelled widely, and while living in Japan for three years had her creative nonfiction published in Canadian newspapers. She lives with her family in the community of Unionville, in Markham, Ontario.

Aprille Janes

Aprille Janes is a writer and workshop facilitator specialising in creativity and writing. Her poetry and fiction have been included in several anthologies and on CBC National Radio. As a freelance writer she is a regular contributor to several large publications. She is a professional member of the CAA and PWAC and served three terms as president of the Writers' Circle of Durham Region as well as a judge for the Mississauga Literary Arts Council Awards.

Irv Haberman

Retirement is great. It provides the time to pursue my keen interest in writing, mainly in the genre of thriller/suspense. The seed was planted when, as a youngster, I read all the books by Ian Fleming. His main character was, of course, James Bond 007. Now, many years later, the seed is trying to bloom and I am relishing the challenge.

Rosanna Battigelli

Rosanna Battigelli was born in Italy and emigrated to Canada in 1963. She is an award-winning teacher and writer living in Sudbury, Ontario. She has received Best Practice Awards from OECTA (Ontario English Catholic Teachers Association) in 2002, 2004 and 2005. She has presented literacy workshops to educators across Ontario. She writes fiction for children and adults. Her stories have appeared in Canadian anthologies, including Mamma Mia! Good Italian Girls Talk Back. (ECW Press, 2004)

For information about the
Canadian Authors Association

Please visit our website:

www.canauthorstoronto.org